SISTER, SISTER

A Babygirl Drama

BABYGIRL DANIELS

Urban Books, LLC
1199 Straight Path
West Babylon, NY 11704

Sister, Sister © copyright 2009 Urban Books, LLC

ISBN- 13: 978-1-60162-154-2
ISBN- 10: 1-60162-154-X

First Printing September 2009
Printed in the United States of America

10   9   8   7   6   5   4   3   2   1

Distributed by Kensington Publishing Corp.
Submit Wholesale Orders to:
Kensington Publishing Corp.
C/O Penguin Group (USA) Inc.
Attention: Order Processing
405 Murray Hill Parkway
East Rutherford, NJ 07073-2316
Phone: 1-800-526-0275
Fax: 1-800-227-9604

SISTER, SISTER

A Babygirl Drama

Chapter One

My name is Tara Evans, and if someone were to examine my life, they would think that I had it good. I live in Southfield, Michigan, which is a nice suburban area right outside of Detroit. My family is what some might consider paid. Both my mother and father work for General Motors, and in Michigan that equaled affluence and success.

Out of all my friends, I'm the only one who has two parents living under the same roof, so I guess some could consider me fortunate, but I didn't quite see it that way. See, I had to share my parents because I was not an only child. I'm a twin, and although everybody thinks it is so cool to have one, let me be the first to tell you it's not.

Physically. My sister Mya and I were identical in every way. We had the same chestnut-colored skin, the same length and texture hair, and the same honey brown eyes. It would seem that since we were so much alike everyone would treat us the same, but I noticed a difference from even my own parents when I was only five.

Mya had always been the popular twin. She was the one that people gravitated to. People liked her and wanted to be around her. They didn't necessarily exclude me, but they only included me because of Mya. Invitations to birthday parties and other social events always had Mya's name on them first. I almost felt like people said, "You might as well invite her sister too."

Even my parents put her first. They catered to her as if she was their little china doll, giving her any and everything that she asked for. Even something so small as Mya sitting in the front seat while I was stuck in the back bothered me. I don't even think my parents realized that they did this, but it didn't stop it from hurting all the same.

They were harder on me than they were on Mya. If I brought home a bad grade from school, then they were down my throat telling me that I could do better, but if Mya happened to slip up once or twice, they were very understanding. It may sound like I'm whining, but I'm not. It was unfair that I had to live in my sister's shadow. I wanted to be my own person for so long that sometimes I just wanted to scream, "WHAT ABOUT ME?"

I felt neglected by my parents, invisible to my friends, and unimportant in general. Mya's life was so great that I couldn't help but feel jealous. Please don't get me wrong. I loved my sister. I could see why everyone worshiped the ground she walked on. She was amazing. Besides being gorgeous, she was confident. She had a diva complex that fit her perfectly, and she dressed as if she had stepped off of the front cover of a magazine. I admired her and wished that we could switch personalities. I wanted what she had. I wanted people to see me and think of me as the "it girl."

Mya was known all the way from Southfield to Inkster. Everyone in and out of Detroit knew her. Even kids from other schools knew who my sister was. Her reputation preceded her, and I wished that I knew what it felt like to be in her shoes.

Summer vacation was winding down and everybody was excited about going back to school. Mya and I had one last thing on the agenda before we could focus on returning to tests and study groups. We had to plan our seventeenth birthday party. Well, Mya did most of the planning because she basically had the entire shindig mapped out in her head before we even sat down with our parents. My mom and dad didn't even notice that Mya was making all the decisions until the entire thing was already planned.

"Ooh, is there something that you want to add, Tara? Everything is already done, but I'm sure we can rearrange some things if you have some ideas," my father said.

"Noo," Mya whined. "If anything gets added, it will take away from the party. It will be perfect, Tara. I promise." Mya turned to me and put her arms around

4

my neck as she kissed my cheek repeatedly. "Please, please just let me plan our party this year. Next year you can do the entire thing—I pinky swear."

It was a pinky swear that she had broken since we were ten years old. Like I said before, she always got her way and I was always left with no opinion or voice of my own.

"It's fine, Daddy," I replied quietly with a disappointed look on my face. "May I be excused?" I asked as I stood.

My mother looked toward my father and then at Mya before responding, "Sure, sweetheart. You're excused. Are you sure you don't have any ideas? I'm sure Mya won't mind if you add just a couple."

Add a couple? I thought angrily. *You didn't give Mya a limit to the amount of things she could add.* "No . . . it's her party; she can plan it." I walked away and had to brush a tear away as I walked to my room.

I don't think that Mya tried to be selfish. I blamed my parents. They had created such a drastic difference between the two of us for so long that everybody assumed Mya was the better twin. They had placed her on an untouchable pedestal, and no matter what I did, I couldn't compete. That was not how a sisterhood was supposed to be. I knew that I shouldn't feel like I had to compete for attention and love with my own sister, but I did.

Mya came bouncing into the room. She sat down on my bed and handed me a long list of names.

"What is this?" I asked dryly.

"The guest list. Daddy said that I had to run it by you," she replied.

I looked over the list. All one hundred names were people that I knew, but most of them were Mya's fans. One name in particular caused a smile to cross my face.

"What are you smiling at?" Mya asked as a wicked smile crossed her own face. "You must be looking at Maurice's name," she teased. "I know you like him."

"I don't like him. I don't even really know him, Mya. I've only seen him around," I insisted. I didn't want Mya to know that I had a school girl's crush on Maurice. He was a young thug around our neighborhood. He was our age, but he rarely went to school. The only time I saw him was when he was

6

trying to show off something new that he had like shoes, jewelry, or a car. I knew that he was bad news. Although my sister and I had permission to date, my parents would never allow me to leave the house with him in a million years. As soon as he pulled up with his old school Monte Carlo and speakers knocking, my daddy would have chased him away without hesitation.

"Yeah okay, Tara. You ain't fooling anybody. I'll hook you up if you want me to. You know he's Asia's half brother," Mya urged on.

"I told you I wasn't feeling him like that, My-My," I said, using the nickname I had given her as a child. "So leave it alone."

"Okay, but when one of these girls out here takes your man from right underneath your nose, don't say I didn't tell you to get on him first." She laughed and snatched the list from my hands. "So, are you gonna add any names or what?"

"No, I think you got it covered. I'll just show up," I stated.

"It's going to be the hottest party of the year!" Mya was excited. I could tell because it was all she had talked about since the beginning of the summer. Now that the party was only a week away, she was like a kid who could not wait for Christmas to arrive. "By the way, what are you wearing?" she asked.

"I don't know. I'm going to just wear something I already have, I guess," I replied nonchalantly. The party had become an all-about-Mya affair. I really didn't think it mattered what I wore. Everything was going to revolve around her anyway. I would be surprised if she put my name on the cake.

"No, you are not going to wear something old. This is our birthday. We have to be the best-dressed girls there. I know you want to look cute for Maurice," she sang as if that would make me change my mind. "You should ask Daddy to buy us new outfits."

"Why me? You're the one who he can't tell no," I stated sarcastically.

"I know, but you have to warm him up. Once he tells you no, he'll think about it for a minute and feel bad. Once I go back and ask him again, he's sure to say yes. So go hurry up and ask him," she urged.

I don't even think she knew exactly how bossy she was. It was just her personality and I was used to it. The fact that my father could tell me no and turn around and tell Mya yes bothered me, but I did want a new outfit, so I went along with Mya's plan.

My parents were sitting in the dining room looking over the bill from the party planner that they had allowed Mya to hire. I sensed something was wrong and that this was the wrong time to be asking for something, but if I went back upstairs, Mya would only usher me back down, so I got it out of the way.

"Daddy," I said. "Can I have some money to buy a new outfit for the party?"

My father stood up and approached me. "Sweetheart, I wish that I could. Things are kind of tight right now. My job is not as stable as it used to be, and your sister has already gone over budget with this party for the two of you. Can you just wear something out of your closet for Daddy?" he asked.

His answer would not have been so heartbreaking if I had not known that he would turn right back around and tell Mya yes. I wondered what was so much better about my sister that made my parents love her more, and my eyes started to tear, but I blinked them away.

"Sure, Daddy, I'll wear something in my closet. I have some cute stuff anyway," I answered.

He kissed my forehead and replied, "That's my girl. I love you, sweetheart."

"I love you too," I replied.

I went back upstairs, and as soon as I entered my room Mya stated, "Did he say no yet, or did he hit you with the 'I'll think about it'?"

"He said no," I answered. "He always says no."

"Okay, well, let me show you how it's done, sis." Mya got up to leave as I sat down on my bed. She didn't know how much it hurt to be the twin that no one cared about. *If she knew what it was like to be me, she wouldn't throw stuff in my face so much,* I thought.

I knew that my sister was not a bad person. Selfish, yes, arrogant, yes, but I couldn't see her intentionally hurting my feelings; at least I hoped she would never do the things that she did on purpose. I crept out of my room and stood at the top of the stairs to see what my father would tell Mya.

"Didn't your sister just ask for a new outfit?" I heard my mother say. "I know she told you what your father said." I knew that they had to be stressed over money because our mother didn't usually speak to Mya in such a harsh tone. She was just as bad, if not worse than Daddy when it came to spoiling my sister.

"That's all right, Monica," my father interrupted my mother. "How much money do you need, Mya?" he asked.

What? My brain screamed in rage and jealousy. When I asked, he was broke. Now just because it was Mya, he suddenly had money. Favoritism was not the word to describe how my father treated us.

"Three hundred," Mya replied. She was so spoiled. She stood with one hand on her hip and the other hand stuck out waiting for our father to place the bills inside. Mya really did act like money grew on trees, and the fact that my parents gave her no limits was a part of the problem.

I watched as my father went into his wallet and pulled out some money. He counted the money and then handed it to Mya. "Here's four hundred," he said. "Two hundred for you and two for your sister. That's the best I can do right now, honey. I'm sorry."

I could not believe my ears. He was actually apologizing to her for not giving her the three hundred dollars she had originally asked for. How bogus was that? He had told me no without hesitating. There was no thinking about it or empty promises. It was like he didn't mind disappointing me, but would do anything to please Mya, and if finances were as tight as he had told me they were, he was willing to put us in the poor house just to buy her a new blouse.

"Thank you, Daddy," Mya said and then ran up the stairs where I stood with my arms folded. She handed two hundred dollars to me. "We're going shopping tomorrow."

"Whoopee," I replied as I rolled my eyes and twirled my finger.

"Well, if you don't want to, you can wear something old and I'll go by myself," she shot back.

"I'm just tired, Mya, that's all. Thanks for getting the money," I said.

We both went into our room and retired for the night. I couldn't believe my father. How could he love one child more than another? It was cruel to me, and the more he and my mother treated Mya like she was better than me, the more I began to believe that it had to be the truth.

Chapter Two

The next day Mya and I picked up our friends, Summer and Asia, before we headed to the mall. We all wanted to look good at the party. It would be the biggest blowout of the year; even better than the party this dude named Mike had thrown earlier this summer. It always was, and our clique had to be the best dressed there. We were all really cool, but I liked Summer best . . . sometimes I liked her even better than my sister.

Summer and I had met through Mya, of course, a year before when she transferred to Cass High. At first, I thought she was just like everybody else who we hung around. She and Mya became fast friends, but a big misunderstanding caused them to fall out and they hadn't been the same since. Ever since then, Summer and I had gotten closer. She was my best friend. In fact, I felt like she was one of my only true friends because she liked me for me and not because of my sister.

We all headed into Somerset Mall. Why Mya drove to the most expensive mall in Michigan was beyond me. We only had $200 each to spend, and at Somerset that would not stretch very far.

"Why didn't you go to Northland Mall?" I asked Mya.

"Because I don't want to be wearing the same stuff that every other ghetto girl is going to be wearing. If we get our outfits from there, then at least five other people will have on our stuff. Can't nobody afford to shop at Somerset," Mya bragged.

"Including y'all," Asia added playfully. "Didn't you say your daddy only gave you a few hundred bucks?"

"Don't worry about me," Mya stated. "You just worry about what you're wearing, because my outfit gon' be on point. I promise you."

I smirked as I watched Summer roll her eyes toward the sky. Everybody in the car was used to

Mya's arrogance. She had to be the most conceited teenage girl in the world. A young girl with a grown woman's attitude, Mya thought she was the next Naomi Campbell, and she treated people almost as badly as the esteemed supermodel. I couldn't understand why people loved her so much and simply put up with me. I tried to be nice and act down to earth. Maybe if I acted like a you know what, then people would like me as much as they did Mya.

We climbed out of the car. Ironically, I rode in the backseat of the car that my parents had purchased for both me and Mya. Yeah, right? She wasn't even willing to share my parents' attention, so I knew her sharing a car was out of the question.

"I think I'm going to walk around for a bit," Summer said as she began to head to the south end of the mall. "Call me on my cell if you guys need to find me."

"Wait up! I'll go with you," I called out.

I walked away with Summer while Asia and Mya headed into the Prada store; Mya with only $200 to her name. Asia, on the other hand, might have had enough in her pocketbook to purchase something from the Prada store. Because her father owned a popular pizza chain, she pretty much kept money. She was cocky with hers; not as cocky as Mya, but still, they made the perfect pair.

"You ready for your party?" Summer asked me.

"Come on now," I said with a weak smile. "It may be my birthday, but you know that this is far from my party."

Most people loved when their birthdays rolled around. It was the one day when they were granted a pass and everything was about them. I never knew what that felt like. Being a twin, I never had anything to myself. I always shared everything with Mya. Our birthday was never about me.

When we were younger, after my mother and father put me to bed, they would give Mya an extra gift. Every year it happened like clockwork. The first year I discovered what they were doing was when I was five. I had gotten up to use the bathroom and heard my mother talking to my sister in their bedroom. When I peeked through the door, I saw them handing her a gift. I was confused because I thought that we had opened all of our birthday presents, but obviously they had saved the best gift for the best girl.

17

I watched my sister open up her present and pull out a gold necklace. My mother had always told me that we were too young to wear jewelry, but I guess her rules didn't apply to Mya. My tiny heart was broken in pieces that night, and it was then that I concluded that my mom and dad loved Mya more.

"Hey, you should enjoy your party too," Summer said. I think she could sense my distress. I was always good at masking my feelings, but I had gotten so comfortable with Summer that I didn't feel the need to lie to her. "It is your birthday."

"Yeah, you're right. It just feels like everything is always about Mya. I'm used to it, though," I admitted.

Summer stopped walking and put her hands on her hips. "I've got an idea," she said excitedly.

"What?"

"Let's forget about your party," she suggested.

"What? You're crazy. Do you know how much money my daddy has put into this thing?" I replied, thinking that her idea was absurd.

"So?" she shot back. "Was any of that money for you? You said that it's always about Mya. So why even show up? Maybe if you decide to spend your birthday somewhere else, then they will finally see that they treat you unfairly."

I thought about it for a moment. I guess it really didn't matter if I went to the party. I could skip it this year. The entire guest list was written by Mya anyway, and I was almost positive that she had planned everything to revolve around her. The entire world revolved around her. *Why not? I deserve to do what I want and be around my real friends on my birthday. Sometimes I have to make things about me,* I thought.

"What are we going to do? Everybody in Detroit will be at the party. Where are we going to go?" I asked.

"Anywhere you want to," Summer replied. "We can go out to eat or just do something small. Whatever we do, it will be about you and only you; not your sister. I'll even bake you a cake."

"I wouldn't be wrong for skipping out on Mya?" I asked unsurely. I did not want my sister to think that I didn't want to be around her. We had never been apart on our birthdays, but I highly doubted that she would even notice.

"You would be right for doing it, T. It's about time

you stopped letting Mya steal your shine, girl. Take one day for yourself. It'll be fun," Summer insisted.

I smiled. It was good to know that I had one person in my life that had my back. The type of friendship I had with her was the same type that I wanted to have with Mya, but I knew that if in seventeen years we had not developed a friendship, we probably never would.

"You would do that for me?" I asked.

"Tara, please. After everything you did for me last year when my sister died—I owe you. You were the only person I could count on. We're friends and that's what friends do for each other," she said as she wrapped her arm around my shoulder. "Now let's go find you an outfit for *your* special day."

It took us two hours to bargain shop and find something in the expensive mall that I could afford. I was grateful for the release. When we were together I didn't feel like the unpopular twin. I just felt like a regular teenage girl. Summer and I were getting ready to sit down for a bite to eat in the food court when my cell phone rang. I checked the caller ID.

"Here's the queen bee now," I said playfully.

"See if they're ready to meet up," Summer said.

"Hello," I answered.

"Hey, Tara," Mya greeted.

"Hey, where are you? Summer and I are almost done. Are you and Asia ready to meet up yet? Did you find something to wear?" I asked.

"Oh yeah, l found something," Mya replied distractedly. I could hear a horn honking in her background noise and I frowned.

"Where are you? What's that noise? It sounds like you're outside," I stated.

"Listen, that's why I called you. I had to leave the mall. Can y'all meet me up the block?" she asked.

"What do you mean you had to leave the mall?" I quizzed.

Summer frowned up her face and asked, "She left us here?"

I put my hand over the receiver of the cell phone and informed Summer of what was going on. "She wants us to meet her up the street." I then removed my hand from the phone. "What's going on?" I asked her. "Just come back and pick us up." Before Mya could respond, three security guards ran up on Summer and me, interrupting my call.

"You need to come with us," one of the guards stated as he grabbed my arm firmly and lifted me from my seat, causing me to drop my phone.

"What are you doing? Come with you for what?" I asked as I snatched my arm away.

Summer jumped up. "Let her go!"

I tried to struggle against the guards, but that only caused them to get rougher. They pulled out mace and sprayed my face. My eyes burned furiously and I went blind temporarily, everything turning gray as my eyes felt like they were having a seizure.

"What did you do that for? What are you doing? She didn't do anything," I heard Summer yell.

"Summer, call my parents!" I yelled as I felt myself being dragged off. The guards pulled me into the security office and sat me in a chair.

"Where is the merchandise that you stole?" they asked me.

"What are you talking about?" I asked. My eyes were watering profusely. I couldn't stop them. They were running like faucets. "My eyes are burning! I need to rinse them out!"

"Water makes it worse. If you tell us what you did

22

with the clothes that you stole, we can let you go. All you have to do is return them and no charges will be pressed," another guard explained.

"Didn't I tell you I don't know what you are talking about," I screamed.

They opened the door and a young, white woman walked into the room. I could barely see her; my eyes were hurting me so badly.

"Is this her?" the guard asked the woman.

"Yeah, that's her. I saw her with my own eyes. The camera system is out this week, so the managers have us watching the entire store closely. She stole the clothes," the woman said in a matter-of-fact tone.

It wasn't until I actually thought about it that I realized that they thought I was Mya. That had to be the only explanation, because the lady sounded positive that she was identifying the right person. She didn't know that I was a twin. It was a case of mistaken identity. That's why Mya and Asia left the mall so abruptly. She almost got caught shoplifting; now here I was taking the fall for something that I didn't do.

I knew that I could not give my sister up. I was

filled with rage that Mya would even leave me at the scene of one of her crimes, but I wouldn't snitch on her. I didn't think that she meant for me to get caught instead of her, but she should have never left the mall without me. That was grimy and inconsiderate in itself, because if the shoe was on the other foot, I would have never left her.

"You know that if you don't cooperate with us the store will press criminal charges. This will go on your criminal record," a guard told me.

I heard them and my heart beat from the intensity inside of the room. There was nothing that I could do but sit there and take the heat. Mya had done me dirty, but I could not bring myself to return the favor. So I sat silently and waited for my parents to arrive. I knew that they would be upset. I had never been in trouble before, so the fact that they would be getting a call like this would come as a complete surprise.

"We need to contact your parents. What is a number where we can reach them?" a guard asked me.

I kept my head down and gave him the number.

The rest of the guards left the room along with the store clerk, leaving me there with the guard who was making the call. I was more afraid of what my parents would think of me than anything else. I hated to disappoint them, even though they always disappointed me. The guard hung up the phone and I looked up at him.

"I didn't get an answer. Now, I'm going to give you one more chance to tell me where you put the merchandise. If you don't, I won't have a choice but to hand you over to the city police. We can't hold you here," the guard stated, trying to play nice.

I remained silent. There was nothing left to say. When the police finally arrived I was handcuffed like a common criminal and taken out of the mall. Summer had been waiting faithfully in the hallway near the security office, and when she saw me being escorted away by the police, she went off.

"Where are you taking her? Wait!" Summer said loudly as she followed the officers.

"Move out of the way, young lady, before we arrest you along with your friend," the cop warned.

Summer stepped off, but I heard her yell, "Tara, I'll contact your parents."

Embarrassed and afraid, I did not reply. I just dropped my head and walked out. I only had one person to blame . . . Mya.

Chapter Three

As I sat inside the holding cell, I cried endlessly. The police were intimidating and mean; I felt like I would never get out of this place. The intense burn in my eyes from being maced had finally subdued to an uncomfortable tingle. It still did not feel good, but it was bearable.

I kept looking up at the wall as if a clock were suddenly going to appear. I wanted to know what time it was because it felt like I had been locked up for hours. I just sat there wondering where my mom and dad were. It should not have taken them this long to come and get me. I bet if it had been their precious Mya in here locked up, they would have been there before she even got out of the mall parking lot.

Speaking of Mya, where was she? I knew for sure that Summer had told her what had happened by now. So why hadn't someone come for me? The more time that passed by, the more frightened I became. I was cold and tired. All I really wanted to do was go home. I know it had to have been at least four hours that had gone by before an officer finally came back and called my name.

"Evans," an officer called out my last name. I stood eagerly and held onto the metal bars.

"Can I go home?" I asked.

The officer nodded and unlocked the bull pen. He pointed toward a hallway that led to a metal door. "Your parents are waiting for you."

His words caused my heart to skip a beat. Although for the last four hours I'd been praying that they'd hurry up and show up to rescue me, now that the time was here, I was nervous. I had no idea what I would say to them. How in the world was I going to explain this mess to them?

I took one step at a time, pausing a little between each one. I was afraid to face my mother and father, and I don't know why, considering I hadn't stolen a thing. Perhaps that's exactly what I should tell my parents; the truth. After all, why should I cover for Mya? She hung me out to dry. Just thinking about it made my head start to throb, and it was at that moment that I decided that I was simply going to tell my mother and father the truth.

I lifted my head and walked out to the waiting area. My heart broke when I saw my mother's face. Her eyes were red as if she had been crying, and my father's expression was stone cold. The look of disappointment on his face was unbearable, not to mention a hint of embarrassment. My eyes began to tear up at the mere expressions alone that covered my parents' faces. I could only imagine the matching thoughts that ran through their heads as well.

I needed to wash those thoughts out of their minds. I needed to wash those looks off of their faces quick, fast and in a hurry. I could only do it by explaining to them, truthfully, who was really at fault here.

I wiped my tears away before they could fall, then took a deep breath. "Daddy, I didn't—" I began to speak, but he interrupted me before I could even finish my first sentence.

"Not right now, Tara. This isn't the time. We will discuss this later," he said sternly. "Right now we have to get back to the hospital."

"The hospital?" I questioned.

"Your sister was in a car accident," he informed me. "Get your things and let's go."

"Daddy, is she okay?" I asked, my tears immediately returning. How could Mya have been in an accident? I had just spoken with her before those guards came and swooped me up. My head began to throb again, but this time it wasn't because I was furious about Mya getting me in trouble. Now I was worried that she was in trouble; that she was laid up in a hospital near death somewhere not knowing if she was going to live or die.

All of my plans to tell my parents about how Mya had, how I saw it, set me up, had gone out of the window. I wasn't even mad at her anymore. At that moment, all I wanted to do was make sure that my sister was okay.

The silent ride to the hospital consumed the car until finally my mother broke it. "Did you take those clothes, Tara?" my mother came right out and asked me. "Did you do what they are accusing you of doing; being a thief?"

My mother's words stung. She spoke as if she had already convicted me of the crime and only wanted to hear me confess it myself.

And now there it was; the question had been asked. Now came the opportunity for me to let my parents know that it was really Mya who had stolen from the mall. That it was their little angel who was the real thief. And why stop there? I could even go on to tell them how I felt they loved her more than they loved me. I could tell them that they treated Mya like a princess and me like a stepchild, but I knew that now was not the right time. Mya was lying in a hospital. I could not tell on her. Again, I couldn't bring myself to hurt Mya in return for the way she had hurt me.

"Answer your mother." My daddy's voice jolted me from my thoughts and I took a deep breath.

"Yes, Ma, I did it," I lied. It was official. I wasn't a thief, but I was sure enough a liar.

"How could you, Tara?" my mother asked with a shaky voice in an attempt to hold back her tears. I could hear just how ashamed of me she was by the tone of her voice. "You know that you don't need to steal anything. We provide you with everything that you need!" my mother yelled at me.

I cried quietly in the back seat. I knew if she had been speaking to Mya that she would not have raised her voice. I even imagined my father chiming in and saying, "Mya, sweetheart, if two hundred dollars wasn't enough for you to get what you wanted, then you should have asked me for more. As a matter of fact, you should have kept your sister's share of the money and just spent it all on yourself."

Yep, that's exactly how the scenario would have panned out had the shoe been on Mya's foot instead of mine. I just couldn't understand it. *Why do my parents hate me so much?* I thought sadly.

My father interrupted my mother's tirade. "Monica, stop it. What's done is done. She did it and she will be punished. Right now we need to focus on Mya. She is the one who needs us right now. Tara will have to wait."

His words were like knives to my heart, and I began to sob uncontrollably. Why did I have to wait? Why couldn't Mya wait sometimes? I've heard that kids sometimes show out and do bad things in order to get their parents' attention. It was obvious that would never work with my parents because even after leading them to believe I had shoplifted from the mall, gotten myself arrested, and could be facing jail time, they still didn't pay me any mind.

We pulled into the emergency parking lot and I slowly climbed out of the car. Animosity was eating at me, but I was worried about Mya as well. I was so emotional that I didn't know how I felt. I was a confused little girl yearning for my parents' acceptance.

We all walked through the hallway and my father instructed my mother and me to sit down while he went to speak with the receptionist. Uncontrollable tears of confusion still ran down my face.

My mother put her arms around me and said, "It's going to be all right."

I nodded as I melted into her arms. I couldn't remember the last time my mother had embraced me in such a way. It felt so good, so natural and sincere. I wanted this moment to last forever.

I heard my father's footsteps and I immediately

looked up to him for answers as he approached. The stress on his face was evident. I guess having two big situations with both of his teenage daughters was weighing heavily on him.

"How is she, Rich?" my mother asked anxiously, quickly removing her arms from around me. Well, it had felt good while it lasted.

"She's alive," my father stated with a long sigh. "The car was totaled. Her leg is broken and she has a couple of bad bruises, but she will be okay."

"Thank God," my mother cried as she stood up and embraced my father.

"Can I see her?" I asked.

"Sure, go ahead. We'll give the two of you a minute alone," my father said.

"Is that a good idea?" my mother asked, releasing my father. She looked at me like I was a poisonous apple or something. She then looked back at my father.

"Why wouldn't it be?" I asked. "I just want to make sure she's okay, Ma." I was defensive. I didn't like how she was acting.

"Sweetheart, go see your sister," my dad stated. "She's in room eight-fourteen."

I walked toward Mya's room and hesitated before walking in. I had to force myself not to be mad at her when I opened the door.

She smiled when she saw me. "Hey," she greeted.

Her leg was elevated in a sling and there were cuts all over her neck and hands. Amazingly, her face was untouched.

"Hey, Mya," I said. "Are you okay?"

"Yeah, I'm okay," she replied. "I was speeding away from the mall and I wasn't paying attention." She made an aching face as if pain had just shot through her or something. "It happened right when I was hanging up with you."

"Where's Asia? Is she hurt?" I asked.

"No. They brought her in to check her out, but she went home a little while ago. She's fine," she informed me.

Neither one of us spoke for a moment, then I cleared my throat and said, "I was arrested, Mya." I paused again, waiting on a reply from her, but she said nothing. "They thought that I was you and they arrested me."

Mya cast her eyes downward. "I'm sorry, Tara. I didn't mean to leave you there like that." She looked back up at me with a genuine look of regret in her eyes. "I panicked and Asia and I just dipped. We were going to wait for you and Summer at the corner, but then the accident happened."

This time it was me who didn't say anything. So Mya spoke again the question that I know had been eating her up inside for the last few hours. "Did you tell Mama and Daddy it was me?"

I rolled my eyes and crossed my arms over my chest. "No, Mya, I didn't. So don't worry; you're still their perfect little angel." I rolled my eyes. "Now they just hate me and think that I stole it. And they think I stole it because when they asked me if I had, I told them yes."

"I'm sorry, Tara. Thank you for covering for me, though. You're the best sister a girl could have," she said.

Too bad you're not, I thought harshly. I turned to leave and said, "I'll send Mommy and Daddy in. You get some rest."

I walked out of the room and waited in the car while my parents comforted their favorite daughter. I was bitter to say the least, and the more I held it inside, the more unhappy I became.

It wasn't fair how they treated me . . . how anyone treated me. It seemed like I was invisible. I could have sat in jail and rotted for all they cared. They probably wouldn't have even missed me; wouldn't have even noticed that I never even came home, as long as their breath of fresh air that goes by the name of Mya came breezing through the door.

As I sat in that backseat, I seriously began to think about running away. I loved my parents more than anything in spite of how they treated me. I couldn't stand for them to be angry with me, and I hated Mya for not stepping up to the plate and admitting that she was the one who had made the bad decision. She was the thief, not me. But leave it to Mya to always put herself first.

I knew that she would milk her injury for all that it was worth. It was just another attention grabber for her. It was another reason for people to treat her kindly and sincerely care for her. I began to believe that even if the roles were reversed, and she had been the one to get arrested, and I was lying in a hospital bed, my parents would find some way to make me feel neglected. They always cared about what happened to her more.

At first I wanted to think that I was just being childish. For years I told myself that I was just jealous, but I wasn't. Everything they did confirmed my suspicions. I was not a priority in their life. I never had been. They never attended my school plays, or came to my awards assemblies, but whenever Mya batted her long, pretty eyelashes they came running.

I lay down in the backseat and let my tears fall as I waited for my parents to come out. I just wanted to go home.

To my parents' happiness, the doctors released Mya from the hospital the very next morning. My mother and I made a big breakfast to welcome her home while my father went to pick her up. We were silent as we moved around each other. I knew that she and Daddy were still upset with me, and I thought that by avoiding the subject matter, I could make everything better, but there was one question that I had to ask my mother.

"Are you mad at me, Mommy?" I asked with tears in my eyes.

I think she could see how badly I needed her because she put her hand over her mouth and whispered, "Oh, baby. I am upset with you, I won't lie, and we will discuss what your punishment should be as a family, but I want you to know one thing. Your father and I love you, Tara. We love you more than life, sweetheart."

Her words did more for me than she would ever know. I buried my head in my mother's bosom and cried my eyes out. She wrapped her arms around me and squeezed me tightly. I felt her lips graze my forehead with a kiss. It was an even more tender hug than the one at the hospital yesterday. It was the kind of hug that I had waited so long for.

It wasn't that my parents never told me they loved me. They said it all the time, but with me, the passion that they used with Mya was always lacking. It was like they always saved a little extra for her.

"We're home!" my father announced.

My mother immediately let me go and ran to check on Mya, who came through the door on crutches.

"I'm so glad you're okay. I love you so so much, little girl," my mother said to Mya as she planted kisses all over her face. "Don't you scare your father and me like that again," she stated.

I wiped my face and placed the plates of food on

the table. My mother had prepared Mya's favorite: chocolate chip pancakes, eggs, and turkey bacon with cheesy hash browns.

"Here, sit down," she said as she pulled out Mya's chair.

I was silent as I sat next to my sister. My parents sat across from us. Finally, in order to break the silence, Mya began telling us all how frightened she was by the car accident. But once she said all there was to say about that, silence once again took over.

"Well . . ." Now it was my father's time to break the silence. "I think now is as good a time as any to discuss what Tara's punishment should be," my father announced as he put down his fork and looked me in the eye. He then looked over at Mya. "If you don't know yet, Mya, your sister stole some clothes from the mall yesterday. She was arrested, which is why we had to leave you at the hospital alone." My father's eyes shot a dose of blame over to me.

"Dad, you don't have to do this right now," Mya reasoned. I could tell that it wasn't that she wanted to delay my punishment; it was just that the guilt was already eating away at her, and she didn't want to have to sit around and hold her peace while I got punished for a crime that she committed. Once again, it was all about self.

"We are going to handle this matter the same way we do everything else—as a family," my father insisted.

I dropped my head in embarrassment. I don't know why I felt bad. Both Mya and I knew that I was innocent.

"I think that you should miss your party," my father stated matter-of-factly.

"Rich!" my mother exclaimed. "Her own party?"

I was surprised that she had taken up for me.

"Dad!" Mya protested as well.

I was even more surprised when my sister objected, seeing how it had pretty much been her own party anyway. I'd think she'd be glad that my father was only making it official.

I couldn't believe that my own father was trying to take my birthday party away from me. Even though I had concluded that I was not going anyway, I was crushed. How could he do that? Why would he do that? It was like he was trying to remove me from the celebration of my birth. If I had

41

a life savings, I would have bet it all that he wished he could take away my birth date for real and only have one daughter . . . the perfect daughter in Mya.

"Rich, isn't that a bit extreme?" my mother asked. "I mean, all of her friends are going to show up expecting to see her."

"No, stealing is extreme, Monica. We raised her better than that," he said sternly. "Tara will miss the party." He shot me a look. "Maybe next time you will think twice before you decide to take something that you can't afford."

I just sat there biting my tongue, trying to hold back my emotions. "Do you have anything to say?" he asked me.

I thought about his question for a few seconds. I had a lot to say. I wanted to cuss and scream and beg him to show some compassion for me. I wanted to go off on my parents and tell them that they had more than one daughter, but I didn't. I shook my head and kept it all inside like I always did.

Mya put her fork down and looked at me in distress, but I knew my sister, and deep in her eyes I could see her jumping for joy. Never mind what her expression and her tone said. A leopard never changes its spots, and if it did, I can guarantee that it didn't happen overnight.

Now she would really be the belle of the ball because she no longer had to share the spotlight. It was all about her, and I was left out in the cold.

I sat in silence and attempted to finish my breakfast, even though I had lost my appetite. I wondered if my parents knew the type of emotional damage that they were causing inside of me. I envied Mya and was beginning to hate myself. I thought that there had to be something wrong with me. There is only so much negativity that a person can take before they crack, and I think I was reaching my breaking point.

Chapter Four

I watched from my bedroom window as all of my classmates and a lot of kids from all over the city entered my backyard, which was where the party was being held. Everyone had spent all morning decorating to Mya's perfection, including me. It was like pouring salt into a wound, forcing me to decorate for a party I wasn't even allowed to attend. I could truly sympathize with how Cinderella must have felt while her wicked stepsisters prepared for the ball; only I was dealing with flesh and blood.

Mya, who ended up getting a brand new Ferragamo outfit from my parents, was looking more stunning than ever in red and white as she greeted all of her guests. The fact that she was on crutches only added to the amount of attention she got, and I was sick to my stomach as I heard the laughter and witnessed the fun times beneath me.

It sucked that I had to stay upstairs away from all the action as punishment for something I did not do. My parents had gone all out with this event. The backyard had been transformed into a mini night club. The pool was sparkling underneath the clear plexi-glass dance floor that they had installed. The DJ was set up on the deck, and there was plenty of food for everyone to enjoy. Everything was decorated in white and gold. It was the biggest party we had ever thrown and I wasn't even invited. It didn't seem like anyone missed me, though. They all danced and joked without even being concerned about me.

I saw Summer walk into the backyard with a box in her hand. Mya waved at her, but Summer didn't wave back. It wasn't because her hands were full with the box; it was because she was too busy scanning the backyard as if she was looking for someone, and I knew that someone was me. When she didn't find me, I saw her go speak to my mom and dad. They pointed toward the house and she kissed them both on the cheek before coming to find me. I was dressed in sweatpants and a T-shirt. My hair was pulled off of my face in a ponytail and my eyes were red and puffy from all the crying I'd been doing all day.

I heard the knock at the door.

"Come in," I said solemnly.

"Happy birthday," Summer stated with a timid smile. She came inside with a small cake in her hand, which must have been what was inside the box. I gave her a weak smile and cleared a spot on my bed for her to sit down. She hugged me. "I haven't heard from you in a week. Every time I call you, your parents say you're unavailable."

"Punishment," I explained.

"Punishment for what, Tara? You didn't do anything. You know your sister took that stuff! Those guards just thought it was you," Summer exclaimed. "Didn't you tell your parents what happened?" Summer thought for a moment and then nodded her head toward the backyard. "Obviously not, since you're the one up here and Mya's the one down

46

there kickin' it like MTV is out there filming the whole party."

"I know . . . I know," I said in a frustrated tone. "I was going to tell them the truth, but then when I found out that Mya got into a bad accident while she was fleeing the scene, I just couldn't. I mean, I didn't know whether my sister was dead or alive. I couldn't tell on her. Believe me, I wanted to, but my parents were so worried about her, I couldn't bring myself to tell them the truth." I folded my legs underneath me and leaned back against my headboard.

"So now she gets to live it up while you are stuck up here by yourself? That's not right, T, and you know it. You should have told your parents the truth. How many times are you going to let her walk all over you?" Summer asked.

I knew what it looked like, but she didn't understand. What if I did stand up for myself? What if I told my parents how I felt about the way they treated Mya and the way that they treated me? I could possibly hear an answer that I wasn't ready for. I did not want my suspicions to be confirmed. I would rather deal with it on my own.

"I don't know, Summer," I responded. "I don't know." I quickly changed the subject. "Did my parents say you could come up?"

"Yeah, I guess they wanted to show you a little bit of sympathy," Summer stated with a laugh. "I thought you were up here getting dressed for our planned mission to ditch this party anyway. Oh well." She sighed as she took two paper plates that she had brought up with her and a plastic fork and knife, then set her home baked confection on my dresser. She pulled a small box from her pocket, and then pulled out seventeen candles from it and stuck them into the icing, and lit them one by one. "Okay, make a wish!"

I got up from the bed and walked slowly over to the dresser and made my wish out loud. Who cares if I went against superstition and said my wish out loud? It probably wasn't going to come true anyway. "I wish everyone would see me for me. I just want to be my own person for once in my life," I wished right before I leaned over and blew out the candles.

"Only you can make that wish come true, Tara," Summer said.

I nodded. "Are you going back to the party?" I knew she would say no. Summer was a great friend like that, which is why I loved her so much.

"Girl, please. This is where the party is at," she said as she got up and went to my radio and turned it on. I laughed at her as she danced to Soulja Boy's latest hit. The old heads might not have thought it was real Hip-Hop, but for my generation, Soulja Boy was what was up.

"What are you doing?" I asked Summer as I chuckled at her miserable attempt to get the dance that went along with the song down pat. "I need to show you how to do this—move over," I stated as I walked up beside her and joined her in the dance craze. I had a mix CD in the stereo and the songs changed from Soulja Boy to Chris Brown to Lil' Mama to T. Pain and many more of my favorite artists. I was grateful for a friend like Summer. What I thought would be the worst birthday of my life actually turned out to be quite fun.

In the midst of Summer and I clownin', I heard a knock at my door and I answered it. I was surprised to see Maurice, my crush, standing in my doorway. Summer noticed who was at the door and her jaw hit the floor. She scrambled to turn down the music. I shifted uncomfortably in my stance because I knew that I looked hit.

"Uumm, I was wondering where the bathroom is?" he asked.

"Oh, it's at the other end of the hall on the right," I said shyly, wondering how he'd managed to pass the guest bathroom downstairs and get all the way upstairs.

He peeked his head into my room and smiled as he looked me up and down. "Why aren't you outside? Isn't it your birthday too? Are you sick or something?"

"No, I'm not sick. It's a long story," I replied. "I'm just chilling in here with my girl, Summer. You know her, right?"

"Yeah, what's good, Summer!" he said as he threw up a peace sign at her. He rubbed the back of his head and looked around nervously. "Your old man ain't gonna shoot me for being up here, is he?"

I laughed. "What he doesn't know can't hurt him, right? You want some cake?" I asked, pointing to the cake that sat on my dresser. "It's not as fancy as the one downstairs, but it's good."

He stepped into my room, his tall frame looming over me. I could not believe he was actually in my room. Summer got up and asked, "Is Asia here?"

Maurice nodded. "She's out back."

"Tara, I'm going to go speak to her. I'll be back in a few." Summer got up and walked out. She hit the lock on my bedroom door on her way out and threw me a sly grin.

I had never been alone with Maurice before. I had never even really spoken to him. We ran in the same circles, but I was never the talk-too-much type of girl, so we had never had a personal conversation.

"So why haven't you ever said anything to me before today?" he asked.

I blushed and lowered my eyes from his. Being so close to him was making me nervous. "What do you mean?" I asked as I went and sat down on my bed.

"I mean, my sister told me you liked me, but I don't get that vibe. You never say anything. Most of the time when you are around, Mya does most of the talking," he responded.

"I guess I never had a reason to talk to you before. Why? Did you want me to talk to you?" I asked with a slight smile.

"I thought you might be a cool girl, but you're shy. You have to get out of that," he said.

I shifted uncomfortably. I couldn't believe that I was so bummy in front of him. I felt like I wanted to die.

He cut himself a piece of cake and stood up while he bit into it. "I'm going to head back to the party. I don't want to get you in no trouble. Happy birthday, shy girl." I stood too so that I could walk him out. "You look beautiful. Next time you see me in the streets, make sure you come talk to me," he instructed.

When he actually bent down and kissed my cheek, I felt like I would die. I couldn't believe that he thought I was pretty. I thought for sure Mya would have been his type over me. After all, she was the more outgoing and vocal one.

"I got you," I said, smiling widely. I couldn't help myself. He had just made my night.

He chuckled and said, "For real, ma, I'm trying to kick it with you sometime. I'll see you on the block." He walked away and I closed my door behind him. Then I raced over to my bed and let out a muffled scream into my pillow. I could not believe that Maurice Davis had just flirted with me.

A couple of minutes later, Summer came rushing into the room with a mischievous look on her face.

"What was that all about?" Summer asked me with anticipation.

"He called me beautiful," I whispered in excitement. "He told me to check for him next time I was around his way."

"What?" Summer rejoiced. "See, you are just as good, if not better than your sister, and that just proved it."

I was so elated that I couldn't stop smiling. Summer and I kicked it for a couple more hours, but when the partygoers began to disperse, she broke out.

When everybody was gone, Mya came up to my room. "Oh my goodness, that was the best birthday I ever had!" she yelled, flopping onto her bed as if she was absolutely exhausted.

I knew she was discreetly trying to rub it in my face, but I did not care. Nothing could have erased the smile on my face. "Yeah, it was the best birthday I ever had too," I shot back.

"What was so great about yours?" she asked in confusion.

"You don't have to know all my business," I replied. "It was just a really good day . . . much better than I could have ever expected." There was this dreamy look in my eyes that I know made me look corny, but I didn't care.

I could tell that my happiness ate at her. She was dying to know what I was talking about and why I was so happy, but I refused to divulge any information.

"Did everything go as you planned?" I asked her.

"Yeah, it went great. I missed you, though," Mya said.

"Honestly, I was actually kind of happy to spend the day to myself. Summer came up and stayed with me during the party and someone else dropped in to wish me happy birthday too, so I'm good," I said.

When I mentioned Summer's name, Mya's jaw tightened. I was beginning to think that Mya only kept Summer around to keep her enemies close. I know my sister like the back of my hand, I knew for a fact that she was intimidated by Summer.

Summer was equally beautiful and wise beyond our teenage years, due to the fact that she grew up fast after her mom died when she was a kid. I reveled in the fact that someone intimidated Mya the way that she intimidated me. Summer usually stole my sister's shine when she was around; the same way that Mya stole mine.

Our parents walked into the room with a serious expression on their faces. "Mya . . . Tara, we need to talk with you both," my father said as he came in and leaned against my dresser. His face was so sad and my mother looked like she had just finished crying. It was almost as if someone had died.

"What's going on?" I asked.

"Your mother and I have had to make some tough decisions in the past couple days, but we think that they will be best for the entire family. We love you girls so much and we have tried our hardest to take care of you and to raise you right. You guys may not have understood everything we have tried to do, and we have made a lot of mistakes in the past . . ." My father's words trailed off.

"Daddy, is this about me shoplifting?" I asked.

My father's eyes teared over and I knew that it had to be much more serious than that. I had never seen my father cry before. He had always appeared to be so strong, and the fact that he was breaking down in front of me and Mya meant that something was horribly wrong.

"Daddy, what's wrong?" Mya asked as she rose up off the bed. I could hear her voice quivering as well as we all waited for my father to continue.

"The two of you have been together for a long time. You are identical twins and you have always had each other to lean on. Your mother and I think it is about time you learned to live individually," he explained.

"What does that mean?" I asked.

My father sighed and replied, "It means we are splitting you up."

"What?" I yelled. My mind couldn't begin to fathom just exactly what my dad meant by that. I mean, he was talking as if Mya and I were Siamese twins and they were finally going to allow us to have the surgery that would separate us.

"Tara, you will go to L.A. to live with your Aunt Tina," my father announced.

Mya's chin dropped to her chest, and her hand went over her mouth in shock. "Mommy, why?" she asked.

I couldn't believe what I was hearing. My parents wanted to get rid of me. They were sending me across the country to get me out of their lives. "Daddy, I don't want to go!" I yelled.

I had imagined so many times what it would be like for my family if I was just to up and be gone. Would they miss me then? Apparently they wanted me up and gone, but I didn't. I know I talked a lot about how bad it was at home sometimes with the way they treated me, but it was still home. I couldn't imagine calling any place else home. My life was here. My school was here. I couldn't leave all those things behind.

I thought about Summer. I couldn't leave her. She was the only friend that I had. How could I leave her behind?

"You have to go, sweetheart," my father whispered.

"Ma! Why are you doing this? Is it because of what happened at the mall?" I could not believe that my parents really hated me that much. My mother couldn't even look me in my face. Her sobs filled the room and she went to my father for comfort. I didn't understand any of this. What did she have to be sad for? She wasn't the one being thrown away like garbage. Wasn't a mother supposed to fight for her child? Why wouldn't mine fight for me?

"Tara, listen to me," my father stated as he got on one knee and took my hand in his. "It has nothing to do with anything that you've done. Your mother and I don't have a choice. We have to send you away for a while. It will be better for you out there. It will give you and your sister space."

"I don't need space," I declared then looked to my sister. "Mya, do you need space?" I asked her. I was surprised to see the tears in her eyes.

"Daddy, I don't want space," she whispered.

"Tara, you got arrested," my mother jumped in and tried to reason. "You could have gotten locked up had your father and I not have made a deal with the store to pay restitution on your behalf. They dropped the charges this time, Tara, but what about next time?"

I couldn't even reply to my mother. Tears just fell from my eyes.

"Tara, look at me," my father ordered.

I tried to look at my father, to look into his eyes to see if I could search out the answer as to why he was doing this to me, but I could barely see him because of the tears that clouded my vision.

"I am your father and I love you very much. I know that you don't understand why your mother and I are doing this, but you have to trust me. I didn't want to say anything to you girls, but I just got laid off at work. Yeah, I get a little severance money and eventually some unemployment, but that's not going to be enough. There's a chance that the layoff is just temporary and that I can possibly get my job back in a few months, but until then, we will be running this household off of one income."

My father could tell by the expression on my face,

and the way I was shaking my head, that I was not accepting his reasoning.

"It won't be forever, sweetheart," he assured me. "We'll see how the first year goes, and if you aren't happy after that, then we will work something out. We will come out to visit you, and we can talk as much as you'd like."

"Why do I have to go? Why me? You're not making Mya go away," I pleaded.

My nose was dripping and I was a mess. I felt like a fool to be begging my own daddy to stay in the home I had grown up in all my life. My heart was broken into a million pieces.

I looked at my mom for help, and she came and sat down on my bed with me. She wrapped her arms around me and whispered, "My sister will take good care of you."

"You're supposed to take care of me," I cried. "You're my mother. You're supposed to be here." I was pulling out all the stops. I didn't care if I had to make my parents feel guilty, as long as they didn't pull me away from my life.

"We are trying to take care of you, Tara. You

have to believe us. We love you," my mom said through tears.

"If you loved me, you wouldn't send me away," I said.

My father stood to his feet and motioned for my mother to stand as well.

"That's it? The conversation is over?" I yelled. "Mya? Please help me! Say something, please."

Mya went to open her mouth, but before she could even speak, my dad said, "Tara, there is nothing that any of us can do to change this situation. This is our only option."

My worst nightmare was coming true. My parents had just proved that they loved Mya more than me, and that I had never mattered to them. I watched as they both began to leave the room.

"We love you both," my father said. He looked at me one last time and I saw a tear roll down his cheek. "You will leave next week so that you can arrive in California before school starts back. It's for the best."

I cried quietly to myself. Mya climbed out of her bed and crawled into mine. "Everything will be okay, T," she tried to comfort me as she rubbed my hair.

For some odd reason, the same sister that I felt that I had to compete with brought me comfort. Her touch was soothing, and at that moment, I loved her. I thought about how we had been brought up. It wasn't her fault that my parents always put her first. She only acted the way that they allowed her to, so I could not be upset with her.

For the first time in years, Mya and I connected like sisters should. We held each other and cried together. We had never been apart a day of our lives. Wherever she went, I went, and vice versa. We were brought into this world only minutes apart, now our parents wanted to put three thousand miles worth of distance between us.

"I love you, Tara," Mya whispered in the most sincere and genuine tone ever.

I looked at my sister's face. It was like looking in a mirror. Even the tiny beauty mark above our lips was the exact same size. It was a shame that our parents could not love us identically.

"I love you too, Mya," I answered.

For a long time I had thought that all of my

problems had been caused by my sister. I had blamed her for things that she could not possibly control. She could be mean sometimes and she was as selfish as they came, but my parents made her that way. The same way that they made me feel insecure and undeserving of their love, they made her feel as if she were better than those around her, including me. They had finally done what I suspected they wanted to do all along—they were getting rid of me, and there was nothing I could do to stop them.

Chapter Five

The day before I was scheduled to leave to go live with my aunt in California was a somber one. I had refused to say anything to my parents or Mya since I found out they were shipping me off to Cali. The only person that I talked to was Summer. She thought that my parents were cold for sending me away, and she even suggested that I run away to come stay with her and her live-in boyfriend, Jus, but I knew that I couldn't. My parents would find me eventually, and it would probably only make the situation worse.

Besides, what could I have possibly accomplished with myself as a runaway? A runaway is just that: someone on the run. I'd have to stay in hiding and

I wouldn't be able to go to school. If the cops picked me up on the streets, I'd only find myself right back downtown again. Why should I add any more heartache to the situation than there already was?

For an entire week, I had moped around the house. I was sad and confused, but more than anything, I was angry. Detroit was all I knew. It was my home, and I felt like I was getting the short end of the stick. As I looked at my bags that were packed in the corner of my bedroom, I shook my head in disgrace. Mya and I had shared our bedroom since we were born, but once I left it would become Mya's territory. She was already making plans with our parents to turn it into her personal haven.

It was funny how my parents claimed to not have enough money to care for both of us, but they had enough to furnish a completely new room for Mya. Instead of MTV's *Pimp My Ride*, it was *Pimp My Room*, and from the sounds of it, Mya was getting everything she wanted. Why my parents never decided to do the whole room makeover before was beyond me. I guess they felt all the new stuff would have been much too good for me to enjoy.

In spite of the reasoning my parents gave me for sending me away, I knew that they were using the fact that my father had been laid off as a scapegoat. People got laid off from work everyday, and families didn't economize by getting rid of one of their kids. They got rid of a car, turned off cable, or something expendable.

I shut down my pity party when I heard the doorbell to our home ring. I stood to look out of my bedroom window. I saw Summer's car sitting out front, and for the first time in days, I smiled. At least I would get to hang out with my girl before I left. I had no clue when the next time I would be coming home to visit, let alone stay. The way my parents made it sound, coming back to Detroit wasn't an option, so I didn't know if I would ever get to see Summer again.

I knew that we both would promise to keep in contact. That's how it always goes when someone moves away. I would promise to call and so would she, but after my plane took off the ground, the promises would be whisked away in the wind. We would not talk because it would become too expensive to talk long distance. The best that we might do is MySpace each other, but we would never be close like we could if I lived in Detroit.

"Tara! Summer's here," my mother yelled from downstairs.

I looked myself over in the floor length mirror and fluffed my curly, long hair. I applied a coat of apple cherry lip gloss and put a jean jacket over my yellow and white American Eagle sundress. My strappy, sling back sandals matched it perfectly, and for the first since I could recall, I felt like a star.

It was odd. I was always comparing myself to Mya, wanting to be just like her, when in actuality I was just like her. I was beautiful; and I smiled as I grabbed my Coach bag and walked down the stairs.

"Hey, girl," I greeted.

"Hey, you ready to go?" Summer asked. "You know I got to show my best friend a good time before you go away."

"You know it," I stated.

My mother frowned and asked, "You're leaving?"

"Yeah, I want to spend some time with Summer before I go," I replied.

I could tell my mother wasn't too fond of the idea of me going out.

"Tara, you don't think that you should be spending time with your family? We would like to spend some time with you as well. You're leaving tomorrow," my mother stated.

Her sudden desire to want to spend time with me almost made me choke. "Why?" I replied. "You're the ones sending me away. Now you don't even want me to say goodbye to my best friend?" My voice was harsh and I stared at my mother in contempt. I had never been disrespectful, but this time I couldn't help it. If my mother really wanted to spend some time with me, then I wouldn't be leaving in the first place.

There was an awkward silence between me and my mother; and Summer stared at us both in shock. She had never seen us face off like this, so I knew she had to be surprised. My father and Mya were out shopping for new stuff to decorate Mya's room, so they were not present to witness the conflict. This also brought on another thought: if my family was so concerned about spending time with me before I left, then why were they out shopping?

"Okay, Tara," my mother said. She looked defeated. "Go have fun with your friends. Just don't stay out too late. You have an early flight to catch in the morning."

"Don't remind me," I muttered as I stormed out of the house.

Summer followed closely behind, and when we were in her car she pulled away quickly. "What was that all about, T? I've never seen you boss up against your moms like that," she said.

"Yeah, well, I'm beginning to think that I need to get away from them after all. This moving to Cali might not be such a bad idea in the end. All they care about is my sister. I hate how they treat me," I admitted.

Summer was quiet, and I knew that she did not know what to say. It didn't matter, though, because there was nothing she could say that would soothe the aching pain my family was causing me.

"Don't worry about me, girl." I decided to perk up. I didn't want my last day with my best friend to be a miserable one. "Let's just have fun. I don't want to think about anyone or anything negative today. This is my last day in the D, so I just want to chill and kick it. Where are we going anyway?"

"Where else?" Summer asked. "Bel-age!"

We rode to the riverside beach and noticed that all of the hot girls and dope boys had come out to sit on the strip. It was the end of the summer and everybody was trying to do it big before winter rolled back around and shut the city down. We parked and got out of the car.

"Is Jus here?" I asked.

"Yeah, he's around here somewhere," Summer stated. "Let's walk around so I can see if I can find him."

We strolled up and down the park getting crazy attention from all of the guys. I wasn't dressed provocatively, but the way the cat calls were coming in, one would have thought I had on a mini-skirt or something. Summer was used to getting this much attention, and she took it in stride as she switched her wide hips around like a pro, walking with the precision of a runway model.

I could barely keep my head held high because I was blushing so badly. My face was flushed and hot. I had never gotten approached in the way that the guys were doing today, and I didn't know how to handle it. Once again, I thought that being out of Mya's shadow just might be a good idea after all.

70

"There go your boy," Summer said as she leaned in to whisper in my ear.

"Who?" I asked as I looked up. I immediately saw Maurice sitting on top of his old school car. His candy paint job gleamed underneath the late August sun, and his black skin glowed. He wore his cargo shorts low on his waist, showing his Calvin Klein boxers to the world. He wore a white wife beater and had a towel draped around his neck. A fitted baseball cap fell over his eyes, and he wore Nike socks with open-toed Nike flip flops. He looked casual and comfortable. To me, he was the finest boy I had ever seen.

There was a group of girls gathered around him laughing giddily and showing everything that they had to get him to look their way. I had never been the type to flaunt my body. There was nothing cute about being loose. I wasn't trying to have my name bounced all over town by different boys. I would rather be shy than nasty any day.

"Hey, Maurice!" Summer called out, her voice ringing sweetly in the air. I knew she had done it on purpose to get him to look my way. I nudged her slightly.

"What are you doing?" I asked. "Why did you call his name?"

"Shut up. You wouldn't have called his name. I see you drooling over that boy. You might as well let him know how you feel," she whispered. "Uh-oh, he's looking. You better wave."

I turned toward him and gave him a shy wave and he gave me a smile and a head nod.

"That's it?" I asked with a frown. "That's all I get?" I turned to Summer in embarrassment. "I should have never listened to you. I'm out here making a fool out of myself. I told you I ain't worried about him like that. He didn't even open his mouth to speak. His girlfriend is probably over there."

"A head nod is all you need," Summer explained. "He can't be out here sweating you in front of all these people. That would make him look like a cake. If he didn't like you, he wouldn't have even given you that. Just chill. He's still watching you."

Instinctively, I looked back.

"Nooo!" Summer snapped under her breath. "You were not supposed to let him know you knew he was watching. You have to play hard to get. Make him chase you, girl," Summer stated with laughter in her voice. "How do you think I got Jus hook, line and sinker? You gotta play this game right, or you lose."

"What? There are too many rules to this mess," I complained. I have to admit that I was becoming a little discouraged. I mean, why bother anyway? Tomorrow I would be leaving town, so I didn't see where it would do me any good to try to strike up anything with Maurice now.

"No, it's just called game, and you need to get you some," Summer said seriously. "Here he comes," she warned as we continued to walk. "I'm going to go find Jus. Meet me at the car when you're ready to go."

"All right," I stated as I stopped walking.

"Hey, what up, ma? I thought I told you to stop being so shy," I heard Maurice say as he stood directly behind me.

"I'm not being shy," I replied as I turned around and placed a hand on my hip.

"Then why are you blushing?" he asked.

"I'm not blushing. It's just hot," I replied. I ran

my hands over my cheeks as if that was going to automatically take away any signs that I really was blushing. "I see you're having a good time."

"It's all right. This isn't really my scene. There are too many people out here," he stated. "I'm more of a low-key type of person, but I'm out here doing the family thing." He pointed to a little girl swinging on the swing set, and I noticed a light-skinned woman wave and he waved back.

"Oh, I'm sorry," I said. "I didn't know you had a daughter. I wouldn't have put you on blast if I knew you were out here with your baby's mother." I began to walk away in complete embarrassment. I had never even pegged, or even heard through the grapevine, that Maurice was a baby daddy. Had I known that up top, I don't even know if I can honestly say I would have taken an interest in him in the first place.

I knew a couple of guys around the way who had kids at an early age; and messing with those guys always meant drama. They always had some crazy teenaged girl as their baby mama who tried to fight any and everybody who tried to talk to their man. I was so straight on that situation. I had never been in a fight a day in my life, and I was not trying to start today.

"Whoa! Whoa! Wait," he said as he grabbed my arm gently. "What are you talking about? That's not my daughter. That's my baby sis and my moms."

I gave a double look at the woman who had waved to Maurice. "Wow! Your mother looks like she's my age," I said as I peered over his shoulder and admired the beauty of the miraculously aging older woman. "I'm sorry for assuming . . ."

"It's all right." He shrugged it off. "You hungry? We've got some food on the grill," he invited.

I looked back over my shoulder for Summer. She was nowhere to be found, so I shrugged my shoulder and said, "Sure. Why not?"

He grabbed my hand and I could hear the disapproving comments of the girls that he had been previously talking to. I became the talk of the strip as I walked away with one of the most popular guys in the hood.

"You sure one of your girlfriends won't get mad?" I asked.

He smirked and put his arm around my shoulder. "Stop talking slick. I don't have any girlfriends, or even one girlfriend, for that matter," he responded. "Unless you trying to apply for the spot." He winked.

I put my head down and he smiled, then lifted it back up. "Come on. Let me introduce you to my moms." We walked across the park and the little girl bolted off of the swing while it was in midair.

"Maurice, Maurice, did you see me jump?" she asked as she ran at him full speed. She could not have been a day older than four. He scooped her up in his arms. She was the cutest little girl that I had ever seen. She was dark-skinned just like her older brother, but her hair was long and fine, flowing to the middle of her back.

"Yeah, I saw you, Jazzy," he replied. "Jaz, this is my friend, Tara. Say hi." He pointed at me.

The little girl put her head on her brother's chest and waved. She then hid her face with her hands. I laughed at her innocent nature.

"She's cute," I complimented.

"Yep, and she's shy—like someone else I know."

He put the little girl down, and then we sat down

at a picnic table where his mother was. If he had not told me, I would have never guessed this woman was his mother. She looked like his older sister maybe, but never his mother.

"Ma, this is my friend, Tara. Tara, this is my mother," he introduced.

"Hello, honey, it's nice to meet you," his mother said, extending her hand to me.

"It's nice to meet you too," I responded by shaking her hand.

"Y'all want something to eat?" she asked. Before we could answer, she kept talking. "Maurice, fix this pretty girl something to eat, boy. Be a gentleman and bring me a rib."

Maurice got up and fixed me a huge plate of food; it was way more than I could eat. I guess he could tell when he saw my eyes bulge at all the food he had piled on my plate.

"You don't have to eat it all," he suggested. "We got some aluminum foil. You can wrap up whatever you don't eat and take it with you."

That sounded all good, but my plate weighed a ton. I swear he had piled enough food on my plate to feed three people. "Are you trying to make me fat?" I asked as I grabbed one of the ribs off of the plate. He grabbed one too.

"Nah, but you're a little skinny. I got to thicken you up," he replied, and then he gave me one of his infamous, sexy little winks.

We ate and laughed with each other as his sister danced around us, listening to every word that we said. I could not believe how at ease I felt with him. He was real cool peoples, and I hated the fact that it had taken me so long to actually get to know him. Mya was usually the one who had all of the boys on her jock, so I wasn't used to having a boy's focus on me. Usually when guys did approach me, they wanted to know if my sister had a boyfriend. It was never about me.

"What are you thinking about?" he asked. I guess he noticed how distracted I was.

"I was just wishing that I had talked to you before today," I responded as I wiped my hands on a paper towel.

"Why do you say that?" he asked.

"I'm leaving tomorrow," I admitted. I shook my

head and looked away in an attempt to avoid becoming emotional.

"Leaving? Where are you going?" he asked as he turned toward me.

"My parents are sending me away to live with my aunt in Cali," I admitted. For some reason I felt like I would miss him or the friendship that we could potentially have.

"Why would they do that? Are you in some kind of trouble or something?" he asked with a frown on his face. "You having problems at home?" He sounded quite anxious to get to the bottom of the reason behind my leaving.

"Of course not," I replied quickly. "I've never done anything wrong in my life. They just don't want me anymore."

"Who is they?" he questioned, grabbing me gently by the arm so that I would look at him in his face. "Who doesn't want you anymore?"

"My mom and dad," I informed him.

Maurice could hear the pain in my voice. Anybody could see that I was hurt, and I think that he felt bad for me. "That can't be true, Tara. They are your parents," he said seriously as he took my hands in his.

"I wish you were right," I whispered. "But it's true; they don't want me. It doesn't surprise me any, though. They have always treated Mya better than me. She's always been their favorite. I feel invisible most of the time. I just never thought they would give me away. I didn't even have a choice in the matter. They came to me with the plane ticket already purchased."

It felt good to be talking about my problems with someone else. Summer was the only one who knew about it. She had been the only person who I trusted with my feelings, but there was something about Maurice that I felt I could trust too.

"I don't see how anybody could not want you," he said. He paused for a moment and then stated, "Well, maybe I can."

I shot him a look of shock.

He chuckled. "You have some barbecue sauce on your face. I mean, who wants someone around with BBQ all over their face?" That was Maurice's attempt to lighten the mood, and it was somewhat working.

80

He pulled my chin to him and kissed the side of my cheek where the BBQ sat. He looked up at me to see my reaction, which was a smile. Seeing that I was pleased with his actions, he said, "And you have some here." He kissed me on my other check. "And there . . ."

I closed my eyes and my breath became shallow as he planted small kisses all over my face.

I felt like I was in a completely new world. It was as if Maurice and I were the only ones who existed. I didn't even think about his mom sitting at the other end of the table. I didn't even care about his little sister being there and all the other people who were around us. After several small pecks, he stopped.

I opened my eyes to find him staring directly into them. "Did you get it all?" I asked, wishing deep down inside that there was just one more spot that he had missed.

"Yeah, I got it, Ma," he whispered before finally kissing me on the lips.

"OOH!" I heard his sister yell out from underneath the picnic table. I had not even known she was under there. "Mama! Maurice is kissing!"

I laughed as I heard his mother yell, "Girl, get out of your brother's business! Get over here and play."

"Thank you for making me feel better," I said to Maurice. "I really wish I could stay."

"Yeah, me too." His tone sounded just as disappointed as mine did.

"Can I ask you something?" I said to him in a serious tone.

"Go for it." He gave me his undivided attention.

"Why did it take you so long to notice me?" I playfully hit his shoulder, breaking the brief tension.

"Your sister was blocking my view. I couldn't see past her ego to get to you," he clowned.

"Hey! That's still my sister," I defended.

"I know, but it just seems like you need to make yourself shine a little more. Correct me if I'm wrong, but you seem content walking in her shadow; like you're going to get sunburned or something if you come out from under her. You should not be living in her shadow, Tara. You're the star. I mean Mya's cool, but I can see that you are a good person. You don't walk all over people; you walk beside them. You treat them as your equal," he said.

His words were kind and softened my heart to him.

"I wish I could stay here," I said with a weak smile. "I don't even know you that well, but I feel like you are one of the few people that I can talk to."

"Yeah, me too, because no matter what you think, you are wanted," he said.

I rolled my eyes. "Oh yeah? By who?"

"By me, ma. I'm feeling you, so if you ever make your way back to the East Coast, then make sure you look me up."

I was about to respond, but before I could speak I heard Summer call my name. I looked back at her and she motioned for me to come on. I sighed. I really did not want to leave Maurice. I was just now getting to know him. I had just found my comfort zone with him and didn't want to leave it. I was digging him now more than ever. I didn't know if I liked him because I was really feeling him or if it was because he was the only person to show me attention, but either way, I was dying to know more about him.

"I've got to go, Maurice," I said sadly. "Thank you for everything."

He stood with me. "You got a number or something where I can reach you?" he asked.

"Nah," I replied. "I don't have a cell phone and I don't know how it's going to be when I move with my aunt. I can take your number, though. It will probably be easier for me to call you."

Maurice asked his mother for a pen and piece of paper. After she retrieved it from her purse, she handed it to Maurice. He then wrote down his number for me. "Make sure you call me, ma, for real," he said. "I want to make sure you're all right."

He kissed me again, and this time I kissed him back. It was my first kiss, but oddly I felt like I knew what I was doing. It was like I had kissed a million and one boys before him, because I wrapped my arms around his neck and enjoyed the moment. I wanted to lock it in my memory. It was the first time I had ever felt wanted, and I would always appreciate him for making me feel special. Reluctantly, I pulled away and waved goodbye as I walked away.

Summer stood watching me in shock with her hands on her hips.

"I know I did not just see what I thought I saw," she exclaimed. "Were you and Maurice just all hugged up?"

"Does it really matter?" I asked with a guilty grin.

"I can't do anything about it. I'm being deported to the West Coast first thing tomorrow."

"Well, at least tell me, is he is a good kisser?" she asked.

"He has the softest lips I have ever felt," I admitted without hesitation.

Summer laughed and gave me a high five. "Shut up, T. Those are the only lips you have ever felt."

"Yeah, I guess you got me there." We laughed as we headed off to her car.

We hopped into her car and drove back to my house. By the time I made it home, it was close to nine in the evening. I was glad that all of the lights were out. I did not want to speak to anyone. At that moment I felt like they were not even my family anymore. And as far as I was concerned, after tomorrow morning, when that plane took off, they wouldn't be.

But I wasn't going to let that get me down, or anyone get me down, for that matter. I had just had the best day of my life and I did not want to ruin it by talking to my mom, or Daddy, or even Mya. They had each other and all I had was me.

"Well, this is it," Summer said as she put the car in park. "I'm gon' miss you, girl."

"I am going to miss you too, Summer. Thank you for being here for me," I replied. "You're the only real friend I have ever had, and I love you like a sister."

Summer and I hugged. "I love you too, Tara. Take care of yourself; and you better call me sometimes. You know I don't give a dang how many miles away you are; we'll always be friends. Got that?"

I nodded my head and got out of the car while Summer reversed out of the driveway. She drove away and I stood in the front yard and watched her as her red tail lights got smaller and smaller until they disappeared; until she disappeared out of my life.

I used my house key to let myself in, but took it off the ring once I was inside and set in on the table near the foyer. I would not be needing it. As of tomorrow, that house would no longer be my home. I sighed and entered my bedroom, where surprisingly, Mya was already asleep. I thought for sure she'd be waiting up to either find out what I had been up to, or to show off all the new stuff Daddy had purchased for her room makeover once I was out of there.

I thanked God for that tiny blessing. The last thing I needed was for her to rub my departure in my face. I picked out some PJs and then headed to the bathroom to clean up and change into them, deciding to shower in the morning. I then went and lay down in my bed and looked around the dark room until finally I fell asleep.

In my dreams I thought of Maurice. I imagined what things might have been like if I was staying. Would he have made me his girl? Would we have become the cutest couple in the hood, taking Jus and Summer's place? Would my sister hate on me because I had snagged the hottest guy at our school? I knew that I would never know the answers to these questions. My fate was already sealed. I could not get to know Maurice because we were young, and on top of that, long distance relationships didn't work. Too many girls would be after him, and eventually he would forget about me and move on to the next.

In a way, I was glad that Maurice and I had not

met earlier. It would have only made my leaving more difficult if I had already been attached to him. Then again, I was not sure that I could hurt any more than I already did. My parents had killed me emotionally by choosing to keep Mya here with them while I was sent away. It was unfair and I was bitter. I was a young, lonely girl with no one to love me except myself.

Chapter Six

The ride to the airport felt weird. I had all of my belongings in the backseat of our family car. I sat beside Mya as I tried to stop my tears from falling down my face. I had made up my mind that I was not going to show my family that they were hurting me, but I could not help it. I had never been away from them. It had always been the four of us, and now they were downsizing our foursome to a threesome. I was the one getting the boot. I was the one who no longer mattered to the Evans family, and it hurt. My father tried to make small talk while my mother eyed me through the rearview mirror. They had to know that I hated them for what they were about to do to me.

"California should be great," my father stated with a false sense of excitement. I knew that he was trying to make me see the best in the situation, but I refused to see anything but the hard facts. "The ocean is beautiful and I know that you'll love it. You have always wanted to see it. Well, actually you have seen it before. We took the two of you out west when you were only three. Do you remember that, Tara?" he asked. "You loved it out there then, and I know you will now."

He was trying to make small talk, but I was not buying it. I had nothing to say to him. My silence must have been enough to at least make him feel guilty because he said, "Sweetheart, don't be mad at us. We love you."

"Then why can't I stay?" I asked as I looked out of the window.

"This is for the best," my mother replied.

Mya gripped my hand and I squeezed hers back. There was a connection between the two of us that only twins could understand. There is a difference in being a twin than being regular siblings. Mya and I came out of the womb together. We did not always act alike, but we thought alike. We could finish each other's sentences, and if Mya was in trouble, I could always feel it inside, which is why I should have known something wasn't kosher about her leaving the mall that day.

When my sister needed me, there was a nagging feeling in my stomach that I could not shake. Most people don't meet their other half until they are married or in love. Mya and I came into this world with our other half. We were not whole unless we were together. We did not always get along, but I don't think it was because we did not love each other. I just think with us always being considered a pair, we simply yearned to know what it felt like to be alone.

Maybe that was why Mya always wanted to be seen . . . because she felt like she needed to be just Mya. Everyone always wanted to lump twins together. Mya and Tara. Tara and Mya. What folks did not realize is that we were two different people, and we needed to be recognized as such. So, instead of being mad at Mya because I was the one leaving, I held her hand and held on to our connection as long as I could because somehow I knew that once I got on that plane, our bond was slowly but surely going to fade away.

We followed the signs to my airline and then my father pulled up to curbside. He popped the trunk and then got out of the car, the rest of the family following his lead. We all filed out of the car. No one spoke, but everyone understood that this was it. My father pulled my luggage out of the trunk.

"We will come in with you and wait in the security line with you," my father stated. "Your mom already checked you in on the Internet last night, so you don't have to wait in line to do that."

How convenient, I thought, rolling my eyes up in my head.

I wiped my swollen eyes. I had been crying since the night before, and my eyes hurt from the strain. They were red and irritated, but my tears were not worth the trouble because they had not changed anything. I was still leaving, and I felt stupid because I was the only one who seemed upset about it.

I shook my head and replied, "No, Daddy, it's okay. I don't want you to wait with me. I have to get used to being alone. I'll be fine."

"You sure, baby?"

"Yes, I'm sure. Besides,"—I pointed to the car—"you can't leave your car parked here anyway."

"Oh, yeah. That's right. But we can always go park the car in the garage."

"Trust me, Dad. I'll be all right."

My father nodded his head. He seemed hurt by the fact that I did not want him to stay, but so what. His hurt could not compare to mine.

"Okay, sweetheart." He kissed the top of my forehead and stared at me for a few seconds before heading back to the car.

"I love you, honey," my mom said as she squeezed me tightly. "I promise to call you every day."

There goes those empty promises, I thought to myself.

"You will have a great time in California. My sister will take good care of you."

"I'll miss you, T," Mya added. "I love you and I can not wait to come visit you."

I gave her a half smile and nodded. "I can not wait to come to visit you. I love you, Mya. Don't forget about me."

"Never," she assured me as she hugged me tightly. "I pinky swear."

I grabbed the handle to my suitcase and pulled it into the airport. I turned around and watched my family file into the car. They drove away without ever looking back, and I silently resented them for that. The least they could have done was turn around and blow me one last kiss.

"Excuse me, Miss. I can help you down here," I heard the counter attendant say.

I turned around with my luggage. "Oh, I'm already checked in," I told her. "My mom did it online."

"Yes, but you still have to check your luggage." She nodded toward my suitcase.

"Oh," I replied as I headed toward her.

She helped me to check my luggage, and then once that was all squared, I had to go wait in the security line, which appeared to be a mile long. I was searched by security and then directed to my gate. Before I boarded the plane, I went to the payphone. I had the urge to speak to someone who may miss me. I called Maurice, who answered right before his voicemail picked up.

"Yo."

"Hi," I whispered. My voice was scratchy from all the crying I had done.

"Who is this?" he asked.

"It's Tara," I replied.

"Oh. What up, ma? I wasn't sure that you would call," he said.

"Me neither," I said with a slight laugh.

"I thought you were leaving town today."

"I am. I'm at the airport now. I just wanted to call you and tell you goodbye. I don't know why I called you, but I just felt like I needed to hear your voice before I boarded, you know?" I asked.

"Yeah, I know, ma. You take care of yourself all right? You're good peoples, Tara. I wish you were staying so that I could get to know you better, but if it's meant to be, then this won't be the last time I hear from you," he said confidently.

"You always make me feel better," I admitted. "Thank you, Maurice. I'll talk to you later. Bye."

"Make sure that you do," he said before hanging up.

I boarded the plane and flopped down into my first class seat. At least they'd had the decency not to put me in coach. I guess if I was going to be given up by my family, then it might as well be first class. I inhaled deeply as I thought of what my new life might be like. I could not believe that I was on my way to California, but it was time for me to stop feeling sorry for myself. What was done was done. Hopefully, I could start new and be the person I always wanted to be. I could just be me without Mya to interfere or make me look bad. New beginnings—new me!

Chapter Seven

Once I arrived at the California Airport, my Aunt Tina met me at the baggage claim. She greeted me with open arms. Her huge smile seemed to be contagious because as soon as I saw her face, I smiled too.

It had been so long since I'd visited her in California that not only didn't I remember the trip itself, I didn't even think I would remember what my aunt looked like. But she was the spitting image of my own mother, so it wasn't hard at all.

"Oh, Tara! You have gotten so big." She released me from the embrace but kept her hands on my shoulders while she took a good, long look at me. "You are beautiful. You have grown to be such a lovely young woman," she cooed in excitement. "I am so glad that you are here."

She sounded genuine, and the amount of love that she showed me felt foreign. She focused on me. She was not looking over my shoulder waiting for Mya to show up. It was all about me.

"Hi, Auntie," I finally greeted in a low, sad voice.

She gave me a puzzled look. "Have you been crying, Tara?" she asked. Before I could respond, she embraced me with another loving hug once again. "Oh, sweetie, everything is going to be fine. I know you are going to miss home at first, but I promise, it will get better as the days go by. You're going to like it here. L.A. is the place to be. There is so much to do here." I knew she was trying to convince me to see the advantages of being in a new city. I was sure that my mother had already told her how badly I had taken the news of being sent out west in the first place.

"I'm sure it will be fine," I said with a fake smile. "I'm just tired," I lied. I wasn't going to be a pain to my aunt. She had taken me in and I was grateful that she had been willing to do that, so I didn't want to bring along my negativity to her.

"Well, let's grab your bags and get out of here."

My aunt and I waited until my luggage came around on the carousel and then we headed outside the terminal door. I followed her to the curb, where she proceeded to hail a cab.

"You don't have a car?" I asked.

"No. I'm working on getting one, though. With the money that your parents are sending me every month, I should be able to get one soon, though, so don't worry. I'll let you drive it as much as you want to. We will have to get your Michigan license switched first. You do have a license, don't you?"

I was too stunned to answer my aunt's question. I was still focused on the earlier statement she had just made. "My mama and daddy are sending you money to take care of me?" I asked.

"Oh, yes. I would have let you stay here for free, but they wanted to help out. They are just sending a few hundred dollars to help me with the bills and stuff. It's nothing for you to worry about," she said. "It ain't like I'm going to go and make you get a job so you can earn your keep." She softly pinched my waist. "Besides, it don't look like you eat much anyway," she joked.

I tried to fake a laugh, but it was barely audible. I was still stuck on the fact that my father, who was crying broke, had straight up lied to me. They hadn't sent me out here because they couldn't afford to keep us together, because if that was the case, he wouldn't have the ends to be sending money to my Aunt Tina every month.

No matter how hard I tried to convince myself, while on that plane, that things could only get better once I arrived in L.A., that wasn't the case at all. They were getting worse even before I could hardly get out of the airport. To be sent away by my parents was one thing, but to now learn that they had paid my aunt to take me out of their hair was another. It was at that moment that I decided that I would forget about them. If they did not want me, then I would not want them. My feelings were crushed and I felt like a child that had been put up for adoption.

Shortly after hopping in a cab, Aunt Tina and I arrived at a tiny white house in the middle of Inglewood. The scenery was so different from Detroit's concrete jungle. Palm trees lined the streets, and the houses were closer together than they were back home. The heat was almost suffocating, but it did not hinder people from being out in the middle of it. Mostly everybody in the neighborhood seemed to be outside. There was a group of people who looked to be around my age standing on the corner. The block looked like something out of *Menace II Society*. Everything seemed so gutter, but in a different way than what was considered hood back east.

When I stepped out of the car, I felt the movement on the block stop. All eyes seemed to be on me, and I felt uncomfortable as I walked toward the house.

"What are they all staring at?" I asked my aunt as we waited for the cabbie to get my luggage from the trunk.

"Your Detroit swagger, sweetheart. You don't look like they do. We have a completely different style out here," my aunt replied. "You will get used to it. It just takes some time to adjust. Once you settle in, I'm sure you will blend in just like that." My aunt snapped her fingers to emphasize her point.

Aunt Tina paid the cabbie, then I headed inside behind her with my luggage in hand. Immediately after stepping through the front door, I noticed

how small the house was. There was only one bedroom and there was barely enough room for me to
turn around without bumping into an end table.
The kitchen did not even have a stove. There was a
hot plate set up in the corner and I saw a couple
roaches running around as if they owned the place.
I was so uncomfortable I wanted to burst into tears,
but I did not want to be rude, so I kept my frustra-
tions inside.

This was not the type of living I was used to. As I
looked around, I knew that in no amount of time
would I ever adjust to this lifestyle. *They should have
just left me at the jail if they were only going to turn
around and send me to another one,* I thought as I eye-
balled the place.

"Auntie, where am I going to sleep?" I asked.

"Oh, yeah." She disappeared into the bedroom
and then returned with a spare blanket and pillow.
"You will sleep right here on the couch. There is a
pullout bed inside. School starts tomorrow, so once
you get settled in, you might want to take it easy so
that you will be ready." While she continued to speak,
she fumbled around in the end table drawer. "Now,
I've already enrolled you. Your new school should

be getting your records from the old school." She pulled out a piece of paper. "Here's your schedule. I'll be at work when you wake up, but the bus stop is two blocks up and the school bus arrives at seven sharp. Don't miss it, okay?" she instructed, all in what seemed like one breath.

"Okay," I agreed as I nodded my understanding.

I couldn't believe how much my world had been downgraded. I had gone from having my own room to sleeping on a nasty, old pullout couch and from having a car that I could drive to and from school, to taking the bus. Back home, my family was living in a huge home, and I was stuck in the roach motel with my crazy aunt that I didn't know from a stranger on the streets.

"I'ma go start getting my stuff ready for work tomorrow. If you're hungry, there is some lunch meat in the fridge and some bread in the bread box on the counter." She turned toward the bedroom but then stopped to share one last thing with me. "The date on the lunch meat might be outdated, but it's still good. A couple months ago I caught it on sale ten packs for ten dollars, so I bought a few and froze them. I just unthawed that pack yesterday, so don't worry. And there is some red Kool-Aid with orange slices in it to drink to wash it all down. Let me know if you need anything else." On that last note, Aunt Tina made her way into her bedroom and closed the door behind her.

I flopped down on the couch and picked up the remote that was sitting on top of the end table next to the couch. I turned on the television and flipped through the channels while my aunt was in her bedroom behind closed doors. My body was tense and my skin crawled as I tried to kill every roach that came near me. I had always heard that the disgusting bugs did not like the light, but here it was daytime and they were all over the place. That goes to show you how bad they were up in this place.

I stood up because I knew that I would never be able to sleep with the bugs crawling around, so I decided to clean. The living room was basically my bedroom, so I had the right to straighten it up a little bit, didn't I? I went into the kitchen and located the cleaning supplies and got started.

I must have swept up a thousand roaches before I got disgusted and frustrated.

"Auntie?" I yelled. "Is there a corner store or a drug store somewhere?"

"Yeah, it's up the block, sweetie. You need a couple of dollars?" she asked. She hurried out of her room and pulled a ten-dollar bill out of her bra then extended the funds to me.

It took everything in me not to turn up my nose at the sweaty bill as I accepted it. "Thanks, Auntie," I mumbled as I practically ran out of the house.

The sticky, humid California air made my jeans and Bob Marley T-shirt stick to my body as I walked. I felt like I had bugs crawling all over me. There was no way I was sleeping in there without getting some Raid or something.

When I arrived at the store, there was a group of kids standing outside of the store. There was weed smoke in the air, and the group of young girls and boys harassed an old woman as she came out of the store. I walked up and attempted to enter the store, but my path was quickly blocked by one of the girls.

"Look at what we have here," she taunted.

I stepped back and put my hands on my hips. I did not want any trouble. All I was trying to do was get what I needed and head back to the house, but the girl in front of me was determined to give me a hard time.

At first glance, she would appear to be harmless, wearing her low rise cargo Capris with a tight-fitting baby tee. Her hair was French braided to the back and her braids hung down her back. Her Hispanic features were also striking. But it was that permanent scowl that was on her face that made her ugly. I noticed to finish off her look, she wore a blue bandana tied around her arm.

"You must be new around here, chica," she surmised, looking me up and down while circling around me. "Look at you with your high heels. Where you from, fancy girl?" she asked in a sarcastic tone of voice once she'd made her way completely around me and then stood back in front of me, once again blocking my path into the store.

"Leave that girl alone, cuz," one of the guys stated, while some of the other girls laughed at my discomfort.

"Well, the least little miss princess can do is state her name," the girl said. She still didn't budge from the doorway.

"Tara," I answered, realizing this chick wasn't going to let up unless I complied with revealing my name to her.

"Well, where you from?" The grill session began. I had a feeling she wasn't going to let me get away with simply stating my name.

"Detroit," I answered, staring her straight in her face. I had to admit, I was a little scared. The fact that I was outnumbered by six girls and even more guys made me nervous. But I refused to allow her to see the fear in my heart, so I stood tall, praying to God my knees didn't buckle as I felt them weaken.

"Well, we don't like stuck-up Detroit girls around these parts," the girl stated. "You need to walk up the block to the next store. You're not getting up in here, chica."

The same guy that spoke up the first time spoke up again. "Jisela! Leave that girl alone. We've got other things to worry about," he said. "You ain't got no beef with her. She ain't even from around here. Let her through."

Jisela gave me the once over while she slowly moved from in front of the doorway. She smacked her lips and stared me up and down as I walked through the door. "Yeah, you're lucky my brother saved you, chica. You're real lucky."

I ignored her, not looking back.

"I'm sure I'll be seeing you again. But you'd better try to stay out of my way, Detroit," were the final words I heard her yell out to me.

I kept my head down as I walked into the store. I had not even been in town for a full day yet and already I had created some enemies. I searched the aisles until I stumbled upon the Raid. I grabbed a large can as well as a couple of other roach prevention methods. After paying for my stuff, I took a deep breath and exited the store. I was able to exhale once I got outside and saw that ol' girl and her crew were nowhere in sight. I picked up my pace and then hightailed it home.

Once I arrived back at my aunt's place, I began to spray the entire house. I didn't want to miss a single corner or crack.

"Girl, what are you out there spraying?" my aunt asked, opening her bedroom door and sniffing. "What is that I smell?"

I had just finished spraying the bathroom and

was exiting it. She looked down and saw the can of bug spray in my hand. She sucked her teeth and then dismissed me with a wave of her hand.

"Girl, them roaches ain't going anywhere. They have been here longer than me. They might as well be on the lease." She laughed and went back into her room and closed her door.

I didn't see a dang thing that was funny. She might have been cool with the unwanted room-mates she'd grown accustomed to, but I couldn't rest my head knowing those things were crawling around the place.

I continued to play exterminator until I was con-fident that the entire can was empty. I located the towels and washcloths in the hall closet so that I could go take a shower. Of course it would have been too much like right for me to have been able to step into a nice clean shower. When I pulled the shower curtain back, I felt like all I needed was a BMX bike to ride along the dirt trail in the shower.

I looked under the bathroom sink and found a can of cleanser and a scrub brush. Not to my sur-prise, the scrub brush looked barely used. I pro-ceeded to wash down the shower the best I could before hopping in and washing up. But even after I stepped out of the shower, I still felt dirty.

I wanted to call my parents so bad and beg them to let me come back home. Heck, I would even get a job and pay my own way if they'd just come get me. There's no way they knew how foul Aunt Tina was living down here. Surely they would have never even considered sending me here. This place looked worse than the group home Summer described that she used to have to live at. I'd take the group home over Aunt Tina's any day.

I mean, Aunt Tina was a nice person and all, but her lifestyle just wasn't for me. I hated it here and I thought about running away, but where would I go in L.A.? I did not know anybody or even know my way around town. If I was going to run away, I should have done it when Summer had suggested back in Detroit. Now I was stuck.

I pulled out the couch, bracing myself for what I might find inside. To my relief I didn't find any bugs hiding inside. I lay down, but I kept the lights on so that I could keep the roaches at bay. I could not close my eyes. Every time I did, they would pop back open and search the walls to make sure that nothing was crawling around me. When I could no longer fight the sleep, it defeated me and took me into my dreams. It was the only place that I was happy, but in the back of my mind I knew it was only temporary. My suffering had just begun, and I wasn't sure if it was ever going to stop.

The next morning, I woke up and got myself ready for school. I had put on skinny Seven jeans, a yellow Aeropostale crew shirt with black flats, and beaded necklaces and bracelets to match. My hair was pulled off my face in a ponytail. I tried to look cute for my first day of school. If it was anything like the schools in Detroit, everybody would be talking about me by the end of the day. I just hoped that all they said was good.

My aunt had told me that the bus stop was just a couple of blocks up, but she hadn't told me which direction. I basically had to go look up and down the street until a group of kids started to form. I assumed that would be the bus stop, so I headed toward where the kids who looked to be around my age began to gather.

As I was making my way toward the group, the bus

cleared the corner, so I had to pick up the pace. By the time I made it to the bus, all of the kids were filing on. I climbed on the bus last as I waited for all of the kids in front of me to find a seat. Once the aisle was pretty much clear, I was able to scan the bus for an empty seat. It was obvious that our stop was the last stop on the route, because pretty much all of the seats were taken.

By the time I spotted a vacant spot, the bus had started moving. I stumbled, trying to keep my balance, back to the empty seat. I pretty much kept my eyes focused on the ground, because the last thing I wanted to do was to trip and fall in front of all these kids, especially on the first day of school. From there on after I'd always be known as the clumsy klutz. Fitting in was going to be hard enough as it was. The last thing I needed was some degrading nickname to haunt me.

Once I made it to my seat, I flopped down with relief. I didn't want to appear stuck up or anything, so I figured the least I could do was speak to the person next to me. I turned toward the geeky-looking nerd that was sitting next to me glaring out of the window. I waited a moment to see if he would ever look my way, but he didn't. Oh well. I tried. I decided to try the person on my other side that was sitting across the aisle from me. I turned to find all eyes on me. Lo and behold, across the aisle were a few familiar faces—one in particular.

"Hey there, Detroit," the familiar voice chimed. "Told you I'd see you again." She leaned into me and in a taunting whisper said, "But I bet you didn't think it would be so soon."

God, what on earth did I ever do to deserve this? I silently asked.

I heard a couple of snickers and looked a couple rows behind the girl to see some of the other girls who had hassled me the previous day at the store.

I turned my attention toward the front of the bus and almost kicked myself when I noticed that I had somehow managed to bypass an empty spot closer toward the front. I didn't want to look like a punk, but at the same time, I was not about to sit back here with those chicks and allow them to harass me all the way to school.

"Hey, girl, I didn't even see you up there," I called out to the girl who was sitting in the seat next to the empty spot I was now making my way to. I flopped down next to the girl and continued my act. "What did you get into this summer?"

The girl looked at me like I was crazy, rolled her eyes, and took on the same position as the boy I'd just been sitting next to had: she glared out of the window, paying me no mind at all. I couldn't have cared less. All I wanted to do was to get away from those troublemaking girls without looking like a coward. And it looked as though it had worked perfectly.

I made a mental note that from here on out I would sit up front to avoid another confrontation with them. I hated the fact that we attended the same school. I just prayed to God that we did not share any of the same classes. There was nothing worse than going to school in fear. Having a knot in my stomach and a dry throat was the worst.

Being the new girl in town was also going to suck because I didn't have anyone to watch my back or to warn me of things that they had heard. It would be me against whoever did not like me, and from the way I was already starting out, I knew that I would not have very many friends.

Now, more than ever, I was starting to miss Mya. I never even thought about what school was going to be like without her. I was so used to her being there with her dominating personality to protect me, that now, being in her shadow didn't seem so bad after all.

Mya may not have been any kind of match for these hardcore-looking chicks, but she had a mouth-piece on her that would have at least made them think twice. I remember one time Mya and our clique had gone to the skating rink. There had been this dude scoping Mya out all night, and he didn't even seem to care that his chick and her female friends were up in the skating rink. Mya being Mya didn't seem to care either when the DJ played a slow song and she went and grabbed his hands, forcing him onto the skating rink with her.

The dude's girl happened to be in the bathroom at the time, but I couldn't help but notice all her girls' heads turn toward the bathroom like a pack of wolves to go tell her. Within seconds, the girl-friend and her clique came storming out of the bathroom. I thought for sure they were going to go charging on the skating floor, but instead they just stood there looking like the Pink Ladies from the movie *Grease.*

The girlfriend had her arms folded, shooting daggers at the couple every time her dude and Mya rolled around. He ignored her, of course, but Mya waving at the girl like they were the best of friends was the icing on the cake. The song ended, and Mya went her way and the dude went his. As luck would have it, the girlfriend and her crew went Mya's way.

As Mya and I headed for the concession stand line, the girlfriend came up behind Mya and tapped her on the shoulder. Before the girl could say a word, Mya grabbed the girl's hand from off her shoulder and turned around, all the while squeezing the living life out of that chick's hand.

Smiling the entire time, Mya said, "Look, sweetie, it was just a skate; get over it. I just got out the joint for manslaughter. After being around nothing but broads for all that time, I was fiending for a little male interaction. Being a sistah and all, I figured you wouldn't mind doing a favor for another sistah and putting your man on loan for a minute.

Now, if you want me to take him permanently, that can be arranged. I mean, look how he's disrespecting you for me. But do yourself a favor and chalk it up as a five minute loss and keep it stepping. 'Cause trust me, I don't mind going back to the joint, if you feel me."

On that note, the girl had the nerve to apologize to Mya for even coming at her, stating that her dude was the one she needed to get at in the first place. The next thing I knew, the girlfriend and her crew had gone on about their business.

Mya burst out laughing as we went and bought two red pops. I failed to find the humor in it all. Knowing those girls would have mopped the floor with her, Mya intentionally brought on the drama, having much faith in her mouthpiece that no harm would come her way. It was like a challenge to Mya, and every time, she came out ahead. Hopefully, in my case I would too.

"Hey, Detroit!" I heard the girl who had been called Jisela yell out, bringing my thoughts back from the skating rink to the present. Hopefully, I pulled some of Mya's game back with me.

Obviously Detroit had become the name I'd be

branded with from now on. I took a deep breath and turned around in my seat. "What?" I asked.

"We don't wear fake jewelry out here. That is played out, chica. If you ain't wearing gold, then you should not wear it at all," she said as she stood up while the bus was moving and came to the front where I was located.

She sat down across from me, even though there were two girls already sitting in the seat. Jisela's reputation obviously preceded her as the girls, without complaint, scrunched over as tightly as they could, leaving her much room on the seat.

Jisela reached over and pulled my necklace from my neck, causing it to break.

"Look, I'm new here and I'm not trying to start beef with you. So don't touch me again," I spat, not really looking for the type of challenge that would have thrilled Mya, but finding myself in one anyway. I continued with my strategy. "I won't say anything to you if you don't say anything to me. Where I'm from, we don't fight over stupid stuff. If you don't like me, then fine, but you really don't know me to judge me," I stated. "Now, if you insist on wanting to fight me, then make sure it's over something worth your while." I stared her down the entire time without even so much as blinking. I couldn't blink. I was afraid that if I did I might miss her fist coming at me and get knocked out.

"Yeah, whatever," she said after sucking her teeth. "Just watch your back," she added as the bus came to a stop.

Yes! I shouted within. Mya's strategy really did work.

I noticed that when the bus arrived at school, all of the other kids waited for Jisela and her crew to get off of the bus before they exited. It was like they were designated to get off first, and from the looks on some of the other kids' faces, I wasn't the only one that the group of girls thought they could bully.

I stepped off of the bus and flung my book bag over my shoulder as I approached the school yard. The vibe of a West Coast high school was completely different than the ones I was used to. None of the girls dressed up like I did. They were all dressed as if they were prepared to fight at any moment; some even dressed baggier than the guys.

My eyes hurt from staring at the hideous plaid shirts that laced the crowd. It was hot as heck, and

I couldn't imagine for the life of me how they could stand to wear the long-sleeve, wooly getup. Those shirts seemed to be a fashion do in California, but in Detroit they were definitely a fashion don't that would get you laughed at. Nobody wore those anymore.

I heard people calling out different sets to different gangs, and I couldn't believe that gangbanging was still the in thing to do out here. Gangs in Michigan had never been too big. I had heard of a lot of gangs in Chicago and California, but I thought that it was a thing of the past. I mean, we had cliques in Detroit, but we didn't form gangs. That was just too played out for my tastes, although I would not dare say it aloud.

After being searched by a metal detector when entering the school building, I barely found my homeroom before the first bell rang. Just my luck, I was in a class with Jisela and a couple of her loyal followers. The only seat left was the one in front of her, so I sighed deeply and made my way toward it. Just as I was about to sit down I felt the chair slide from underneath me, and the next thing I knew, I was on the floor and my new class-mates were in fits of laughter.

I guess I'd be branded the clumsy klutz after all. I was so embarrassed, but I knew that it had not been an accident. Jisela had pulled my chair from underneath me. My face turned red and I got up and ran out of the room. I had never been a clumsy girl, and I should have known not to sit around that girl. I should have just picked up the chair and moved it across the room somewhere.

I was definitely in a different environment. No-body at my old school would have even pulled a cruel joke like that. The teacher would have had them down at the office so fast it wouldn't have been funny. But the teachers here were probably scared to death of these little gangbangers, and I couldn't say that I blamed them.

I found my way to the nearest bathroom and charged into the first stall that came into view. I sat down on the toilet lid and cried my eyes out. The embarrassment was only part of the reason why I was so upset. The roaches, the abandonment that I felt, and the cruelty of my peers . . . it all added to the emotional breakdown that I was having. I stayed in that bathroom all day and skipped my first day of classes. I did not want to face anyone, and after the day ended, I waited thirty extra minutes so that I would not have to catch the bus home with those same girls.

I ended up walking six miles home, and by the time I arrived, I was too exhausted to fight off the roaches. All I wanted was to rest. I decided I may as well get used to the misery, because it was not going anywhere, and I was here to stay.

Chapter Eight

I hated school, and I hated California even more. You would think that since my entire life had changed and I had not only changed schools, but states, that the way people treated me would change too, but it had not. By getting on Jisela's bad side, I had sealed my fate at my new school. No one would even talk to me. I suppose they didn't want to get caught up in her wrath by associating with me. So in turn, my social status was even worse here in Cali than it had been in Detroit. At least back home people did not treat me like crap. They at least tolerated me because of Mya.

I had been living with Aunt Tina for almost two months now, and I had not spoken to my family at all. No one even called to make sure that I had arrived safe and sound. My aunt eventually called her sister from work one day and talked to her, but I wasn't about to call home first. How could they not call and check on me? On a couple occasions, my aunt had even talked to them from the house, and every time I heard her about to end the call, my heart pace would pick up. I'd wait in anticipation to see if just once they'd ask her to put me on the phone, but it never happened. Not once. So in honor of the standoff, since they never asked to speak to me, I never asked to speak to them.

It was as if I did not exist. I guess the old saying "out of sight, out of mind" was true, because now that I was not around, they truly acted as if they only had one daughter.

My Auntie Tina was cool when she was home, but she worked a lot during the day, and at night she always went out to Happy Hour, bar hopping all over town. My life was lonely and depressing. I couldn't call Summer because my aunt said it would run up her phone bill and she couldn't afford a whole bunch of long distance charges.

I had not even thought about calling Maurice. I

was almost positive that some hoochie mama had snatched him up. I mean, why would he wait for me? I was never coming back anyway.

I hoped that for Thanksgiving break my family would fly me back home. Even if I was only there for a few days, it was better than nothing. I would give anything to sleep in a clean house again. Aunt Tina's house had gotten a whole lot better since I had been there, but I still squashed the occasional roach now and then.

Being in California, it took me a while to adjust to the culture change. I wasn't familiar with the entire gang atmosphere, so when I was jumped for wearing the wrong colors, it scared me to the point where I refused to go to school. I had worn a cute little red top, which just happened to be the color for the national Bloods gang. It wouldn't have been so bad if I hadn't worn the shirt on a Crip block. I received the beat down of my life. One would have thought it was my gang initiation. I was left with bruises for days.

After that incident, I became more and more depressed. My aunt began to notice the change in my demeanor. At first she thought that it was just normal feelings of being left out, but when I stopped speaking altogether, she knew there was something seriously wrong with me.

"Tara, sweetheart, you have to get up and go to school today," she said as she prepared to leave for work. I heard her, but I pretended that I was still asleep so that I would not have to face her. Even though I knew she loved me, I had begun to resent her too for even agreeing for me to come out here. What type of grown woman in their right mind would volunteer to raise someone else's kids in the middle of a gang-run neighborhood, in a roach-infested house? Yes, I blamed her for my misery too. At the rate I was going, I was mad at the world and couldn't have cared less. "I know you hear me, Tara. Get up. You're going to school."

"Auntie, I don't want to go to school. I still don't feel up to it," I whispered in a groggy tone.

"When will you ever feel up to it, Tara? You have been here for two months now and you are still moping around this house. You have been acting the same way since you got here."

"I just miss my family. I miss my sister and Mama

and Daddy. Why did they send me out here by my-self? How could they do this to me, Auntie? I just want to be with them. I want to go back home," I cried. "It's nothing against you personally, Auntie, but I'm miserable here."

Aunt Tina sighed as she sat on the pullout bed and stroked my hair. "I know that you are sad, sweetheart, but you are making yourself sick. You have to start seeing the good in situations instead of the bad. Come on, get up.

"I know we haven't spent much time together since you've been here, so I am calling in to work today. We are going to hang out. Perhaps I can show you a different side of California, other than what you see in just our little neighborhood and school," she suggested. "Besides, it will give us a chance to talk. I want to know what's in that head of yours." She smiled while gently nudging my forehead with her index finger.

"Really?" I asked. "Can we go to the ocean?" I had been there for too long not to know what the water looked like and smelled like. Aunt Tina was right; I hadn't been any farther than my school and back. There had to be another side of the great state of California that I was missing.

"Yeah, really, now get up and let's go," she responded with a smile.

I arose and dressed quickly, then we headed out. We caught a cab to Santa Monica and I immediately fell in love with the little city. It was gorgeous and it was exactly what I thought California would be like. The rolling waves of the ocean were melodic as they crashed into the shore, and the sun glistened off of the water. It stretched as far as the eye could see. It was an endless paradise, and everyone on the beach seemed happy, displaying smiles and laughter.

The pier was huge and entertaining. There was so much to do and so many things to see that this side of the city made me forget my troubles for a little while. We rode the amusement rides and purchased souvenirs. I was like a little kid in a candy store as I explored from one end of the beach to the other.

"Hey, are you hungry?" my aunt asked. "We have not eaten all day."

"Yeah, I guess I am. I have been having so much

fun that I forgot all about food, I guess," I replied. If every day could have been like that, then I would never ever complain about California again, but it wasn't. The California that I received was cruel, and I hated being there.

My aunt and I stopped off at this little spot and grabbed some burgers, fries, and milkshakes. She took this time to, as she put it, find out what was in that head of mine.

"Why are you so miserable here?" my aunt asked.

"I just miss my family. It feels like they deserted me," I finally admitted.

"They didn't desert you. They just want the best for you, Tara. You are their daughter and your mom and dad worship the ground you walk on," she said in my parents' support.

A tear fell from my eye and I swiped it away quickly. My aunt caressed my face with a gentle touch.

"I don't want you to be unhappy out here, Tara. We all love you and you have to know that. I'm going to call my sister and see if they can come out here to visit us for Thanksgiving. Maybe seeing them will make you feel a little bit better."

"I'd rather go home to visit," I told her. "Again,

Aunt Tara, it's nothing against you. I just miss home."

"I think going home right now will only make it harder for you when it's time to come back," my aunt reasoned. "So, like I said, let me call your mom and see what I can do about getting them to come here to visit you."

"They won't come," I told her, not sounding the least bit hopeful.

"Yes, they will, sweetheart. You need them right now, and I am going to make sure that they know it. If you start going back to school until Thanksgiving, then I will make sure that you have the best holiday ever, okay?" she said in a tone as if she was negotiating with me.

I knew that she was willing to try anything to get me to go back to school, and the offer that she was making was worth me getting a beat down every day if I had to. If I couldn't get back to Detroit for the Thanksgiving holiday, then maybe getting my family here was my next best option. That way I could get them to see just how I was living down here and talk them into letting me come home. Surely after they witnessed firsthand the roach motel and gang-infested neighborhood I was living in, they'd want me out of this environment quick, fast and in a hurry. They would have no choice but to see just how bad off I was.

I nodded my head in agreement and replied, "Deal."

My aunt smiled and embraced me as we sat on the beach. I could not wait for Thanksgiving. It would be so hard getting through the next few weeks. But Lord knows I couldn't wait for my parents to see how I was living. I was confident that when they saw all that I'd been going through, they'd be flying me back home with them. As a matter of fact, I was so confident that I couldn't even wait to leave the beach and get back to my aunt's place so I could start packing!

Chapter Nine

I waited anxiously for my sister to arrive. Something had come up with my parents, so they had not been able to make the trip to California for Thanksgiving break, but they still went ahead and sent Mya by herself. I was upset that I would not get to see my whole family, but excited that Mya was coming to town. I figured she could always relay the message back to our mom and dad that I was miserable. Once their little angel got off the plane begging for me to be able to come back home after living in such deplorable conditions herself, I'd be on the next thing smoking out of L.A.

My aunt and I stood side by side at baggage claim. I could not stand still. I kept pacing back and forth as we waited for Mya to emerge through the massive crowd. After what felt like an eternity, I saw my mirror image coming our way.

"Mya!" I yelled and waved my hand in the air to get her attention. She turned her head in my direction and a huge smile spread across both of our faces. I took off full speed and so did she. We practically collided into each other as we hugged. "I'm so happy to see you."

"Me too. I missed you, Tara. It's not the same at home without you," she replied through tears. We cried happy tears as we hugged for about five minutes straight.

I was relieved to know that she had missed me as much as I had her. Standing there in the airport, I felt closer to her than I had ever felt. We were both just happy to be in each other's presence again. Aunt Tina walked up with a suitcase in her hand that matched the carry-on Mya had on her arm.

"Here is your luggage, Mya. I grabbed it off the carousel when I saw that it matched the bag you were carrying. I double checked the name tag on it too." Aunt Tina set the bag down and then opened her arms wide. "Now, come and show me some love." Her arms were outstretched and Mya hugged her briefly.

"Hey, Auntie, how have you been?" Mya asked.

"I have been good, honey . . . just fine," Aunt Tina replied. She stood back and admired us. I could tell that she was trying to find a way to distinguish us from one another. "It is amazing how alike the two of you look. You are beautiful girls. I am going to have to put name tags on you just to tell you apart."

"Nobody back home can tell us apart. I even think Daddy has a hard time. It's a good thing we don't act alike, because we would basically be the same person," Mya stated.

We took a cab back to the house, and during the ride, Mya was in awe of how great L.A. looked as we drove through town. Even the small things seemed to amaze her. She was completely in love with the palm trees.

"You get used to them after a while," I said. "Trust me, sis, it's not as great as you think it is. I would take Detroit over this place any day."

"Then you are crazy," Mya said.

"Tara just has to loosen up a bit," our aunt interrupted. "Once she stops comparing everything here to what you guys have back in Detroit, she will enjoy it better. This is the city where dreams come true," Aunt Tina added.

"More like nightmares," I muttered.

When the cab driver pulled up at the house, Aunt Tina paid the cabbie and got Mya's luggage, then headed straight inside, while Mya and I lingered outside. Mya had insisted on taking in as much as she could for the few days she would be in town.

Just like when I arrived, the entire block seemed to freeze when they saw Mya step out of the car. Everybody wanted to get a look at her. I suppose they were surprised that there were two of me, because I had never mentioned to anyone that I had a sister, let alone an identical twin. But then again, there wasn't really anyone to mention it to.

Mya looked up at the house and I could see a judgmental expression cross her face. "This is it? This is where you have been living?" she asked with her nose twisted up in the air.

"Yep, this is it," I confirmed. "Some paradise, huh? Not even if the entire street was covered with palm trees would make it any better." I allowed Mya to take in the block while a slight smirk rested on my face. "So what do you think of the city of dreams now? Huh, sis?"

For a moment, Mya was speechless, which is a very rare thing. Finally she fixed her mouth to answer me. "You're in the middle of the hood," she commented. "Auntie's house looks like a dump." Then all of a sudden, Mya's twisted up face straightened out with a smile. "But I bet you all the young hustlers be around here, don't they?" Her tone went from condescending to impressed when she thought of the guys and the paper that was probably lacing their pockets. It was just like Mya to have boys on the brain. "You're going to have to show me around."

I could not believe the enthusiasm in Mya's voice. The fact that she didn't have to live here forever was why it didn't seem so bad to her, but I bet if she had been sent to live here she would be appalled. When I looked at Mya and saw the smile that anticipated what California life in the hood might have to offer her, I knew I could forget about her going home and telling Mom and Dad how awful it was.

"There's not really much to see," I told Mya, hoping to deflate some of that excitement she was filled with. "I haven't been around that much. If I'm not at school, then I'm at home. Most of the people our age just hang out on the block. A lot of them are a part of the Crips. I had a couple of arguments and fights with this group of girls from around the way, so I just keep to myself," I admitted.

I wanted to give her all of the dirt. I didn't have much time to change her perception of where and how I was living. The more I gave her all the bad reports, the more she might tell our parents that I was not safe in California and they would send for me immediately. I knew it was selfish of me, but I was on a mission.

"The Crips? They be banging out here?" she asked.

I nodded. "Yeah, that's real big here. They take it pretty seriously, too, so I hope you didn't pack anything red."

My sister's eyebrows furrowed in distress and she replied, "If I did, then I'm not wearing it."

We went inside and she caught me up on all of the things that were going on back home. She filled me in on everybody's drama. I wanted to know who was kicking it with whom, who had gotten knocked up, and who had broken up since I had left. It felt so good to be back in the loop.

"So what's popping around here?" she asked. "What is there to do around here? You know I did not come all the way out here to sit in this house," she said, looking around in disgust, as if the walls were closing in on her.

I wanted to show Mya a good time, but I did not want her to know that I was like a social pariah in California. I had heard a few kids talking about a pier party that would be going on along one of the local beaches, but I was afraid to show up. If I went and ran into Jisela and her clique, then they would make me look stupid in front of Mya. But this was pretty much my only chance to show Mya that I could be just as popular as her—even if it was a lie.

"There is a party tonight on the beach we can go

to. It's supposed to be a big deal. We can go there," I said nonchalantly, like being invited and going to beach parties was an everyday thing for me.

"Cool, let's go. I'm about to get ready," she said as she hopped up.

Three hours later, we were headed for the beach. I was nervous and my heart was beating out of my chest. I just wanted the night to go smoothly. Mya and I wore matching Donna Karan two-piece swimsuits with cut-off jean shorts to cover up our bottoms. Mya had brought the swimsuit down as a gift for me. She said when she saw it in the store, she knew we had to play the Double Mint twins in them while in Cali together.

I was thankful for the gesture, because we did look hot in our little getup. The only thing that distinguished us apart was the gold nameplate necklaces that hung around our necks.

We cabbed it over to the beach, and the giddy laughter of the kids could be heard as we exited the cab and made our way onto the beach scene. Surprisingly, I was excited as I climbed down the sandy beach and approached the huge bonfire that was going on. Everybody watched us as we passed by.

I saw Jisela standing around with her crew. I attempted to turn and walk the other way when she yelled, "Detroit!"

"Great," I mumbled under my breath.

"You, Detroit!" she yelled out again as she came over to us. "What are you doin' here? Nobody invited you," she said, looking both Mya and myself up and down. At first I could tell she didn't know which one was me, but then her eyes caught my necklace and she fixed her eyes on me and me alone.

Mya was always the feisty type, and she immediately came to my defense. "Ain't this public property? Because unless you own this beach, we don't need an invitation."

I thought Jisela was going to go off, but she just looked at us back and forth. "Who are you supposed to be, her carbon copy?" Jisela asked as she got a little chuckle from her girls that had followed her over to us.

"I'm Mya, her sister. I'm from the D," Mya replied with confidence.

"Tara didn't tell us she had a twin," Jisela replied,

taking some of the edge off of her voice. I was shocked. It was the first time that she had actually called me by my real name.

"Well, she does," Mya stated matter-of-factly. "And I did not come all the way from Detroit to beef out with nobody. I'm trying to have fun. What is there to do around here anyway?"

I couldn't believe the way Mya was talking to Jisela like we were all going to hang out together or something. Couldn't she tell this was my arch enemy? Didn't it go without saying that these were the chicks that had been giving me trouble? I relaxed, knowing that Jisela wasn't going to be befriended that easy.

Jisela smiled and put her arm around my sister's shoulder. "Come on, let me introduce you to the crew," she said. Her words were like a smack to my face. How could she be so willing to accept Mya, but she had hated me from the very second she laid eyes on me?

"Come on, T!" Mya yelled as she was dragged away by Jisela.

I walked behind them and took my place as the third wheel. Mya cliqued immediately with everyone there. Everybody thought she was so cool. They hung on to her every word as she told them stories about Detroit. In between stories, they would compliment her on the outfit she was wearing, even though we wore exactly the same thing. I was completely floored. I hated it. No matter where we went, Mya was always going to have the life that I wanted. She was simply the better twin, and it was time I just accepted that fact. No matter what coast we were on, that was evidently one thing that was not going to change.

I admired Mya so much for being able to adapt so easily to a new environment, but I envied her as well. All I wanted was to be like her. As Mya entertained and made sure that everyone's eyes were always on her, I crept off into the shadows at the other end of the beach. I didn't feel like being around everyone else at that moment. I sat down on the sand and wrote my name in the moist earth as my tears wet my face. Whatever it was about me that people hated, I wished that I could change it. I needed to find a place where I could be happy. I looked up and saw a shadow coming toward me.

"Tara!" I heard my sister call out.

"I'm over here," I yelled back. She came over to me, and when I saw her face, I was green with jealousy. I loved her and she was beautiful, but for some reason, when I looked in the mirror, I didn't see the same beauty within myself.

"I know where you are, but what are you doing all the way over here?" she asked as she took a seat beside me. "Why do you always seclude yourself?"

"I don't. You don't know how it feels to be me, Mya," I said sadly as the tears ran down my face. "I am always the one on the outside looking in. I love you so much. You are my sister, but sometimes I can't help but to be jealous of you. You have everything. Everybody likes you. How can people dislike me so much when we look just alike? Those same girls over there that just embraced you, they hated me from the first day I got here. I would do anything to know what it feels like to be you."

Mya hugged me tightly and wiped the tears from my face. "I never knew you felt that way," Mya said. "I love you, Tara. I would never do anything to hurt you. You say you want to be like me, but you are like me. Don't you see that? We are twins, girl. You are just as beautiful as I am. You just have to have

confidence in yourself, T. You have to stop thinking of yourself as the ugly duckling. If you start be-
lieving in yourself, then so will everybody else. It's
all about attitude.

"The first thing people see when I enter a room
isn't me, it's my attitude. I try my best to exuberate
confidence, a confidence that people know they
couldn't knock down if they tried. But you,"—she
pointed at me—"I hate to say it, Tara, but sometimes
you make yourself an easy target."

"It's not as easy as you think to walk around with
all the confidence in the world, Mya, especially
when you've been raised like I have."

"Stop the press," Mya said, putting her hand up.
"That's bogus, because need I remind you, you've
only been living in California for a few months.
You were raised with me and like me."

I sucked my teeth. "Are you blind or something,
Mya? I mean seriously, have you not seen that even
Mommy and Daddy treat you better than they do
me? Think about it!" I yelled dramatically. "They
sent me all the way out here just to get rid of me!
You think I'm overreacting, but no one wants me
around."

Our heart to heart was interrupted by Jisela. "Hey, Mya! Come back over here," she yelled.

"Give me just a minute!" Mya yelled back. She sighed deeply and looked me in the eyes. She took her necklace from around her neck. "Hand me your necklace."

"What?" I asked.

"Give me your necklace. I'll wear yours and you can wear mine. You want to know what it's like to be me, so I'm going to let you see firsthand. We can trade lives for the night," she said as she helped me unclasp my necklace. "Once you see that they like you when you are wearing my necklace, maybe you can start to make them like you when you're wearing your own." She slid her necklace around my neck.

"Thanks, Mya," I said gratefully as we both stood up. I placed Mya's necklace around myself and felt like a whole new person; I felt like Mya.

"Now, let's get back to the party," she said.

We rejoined the rest of the group and I immediately noticed the difference. Everybody gravitated toward me because they thought that I was Mya, and it felt great to be the center of attention for once. I looked over toward my sister, who sat alone on the sand near the bonfire. She winked at me as she watched me revel in the moment. I saw Jisela in an entirely new light. It was like she was fun and vibrant now that I was seeing her through Mya's eyes. I did not act any differently, yet they treated me better just because I had stepped into a new pair of shoes.

I enjoyed the rest of the night. I danced and joked. I was proud of myself for letting all of my fears go for the time being. I showed a side of my personality that I did not know I had. Maybe I could be just as outgoing as Mya.

Everything was perfect until I heard the sound of gunshots slice through the air.

Pow! Pow! Pow! Pow!

I ducked down and covered my ears. I could hear screams around me and then more gunfire.

Pow! Pow! Pow! Pow!

I was too afraid to look up, so I stayed curled near the ground until the sound of screeching tires and gunfire ceased.

"Oh, my God! Yo, she's been shot! Somebody call an ambulance!" someone yelled out.

I finally stood to my feet and looked frantically toward the crowd of people. "Oh, my God! No!" I screamed as I ran full speed, pushing the crowd out of the way as I made my way to the figure on the ground.

When I reached the center of the circle, I saw Mya sprawled out on the sand. I would have thought that she was sleeping if it weren't for the bullet holes and blood. Her face looked so peaceful. I fell to my knees and tried to wake her up. "Get up! Please, somebody help me!" I cried.

Jisela and her friends stood over us with regret and remorse written all over their faces as they watched me try to save my sister. Police sirens could be heard in the distance, and the group of young gangbangers began to flee in all directions. Jisela kneeled and tried to pull me away. "Come on, Mya," she said. "Let's go! The police are on the way. There is nothing that you can do for your sister now!"

Mya. She thinks I'm Mya, I thought as I touched the necklace on my neck. I looked down at my sister. "I can't leave her," I whispered.

Jisela looked as if she were hesitant to leave, but

when she saw the flashing lights from the police car, she ran down the beach.

"I'm so sorry, Mya," I cried. "I am so sorry." I held my sister in my arms as I rocked her back and forth. My sobs were so loud that I was sure I could be heard all up and down the coastline. The pain that I felt was so intense it was worse than anything I had ever felt. I had just lost my sister and I could feel the hole begin to form in my heart. My body burned in every place where Mya had been shot. It was as if I shared in her death, and at that moment, I truly believed that a part of me had died too.

Chapter Ten

I don't know how it happened. Everyone just assumed that I was Mya, and I allowed them to believe it. I allowed them to believe that I, Tara Evans, was dead, when it was my identical twin sister Mya who had really died.

One tiny piece of jewelry had changed my identity in the blink of an eye, and now I finally had my chance to actually know what it was like to be in my sister's shoes. I guess the saying is true: Be careful what you ask for—you just might get it.

I know I should have told someone that they were making a drastic mistake by thinking it was my name that belonged on a death certificate, a headstone, but I couldn't. My parents loved Mya more than me, and if they ever found out that she was really dead, then they would blame me, possibly hating me even more than they already did. This was my chance to get my parents' love and to go back to Detroit.

When the police had first arrived on the scene, they couldn't pry my sister out of my arms, and when they finally did, I was so hysterical that they had to put me in an ambulance and send me to the hospital. The nurses gave me a sedative that numbed me to the pain and knocked me out before I could get a chance to explain my true identity. I must have been out cold for a while, because when I awoke, my parents were already there.

"Mya, sweetheart, we are here for you," they whispered in my ear as they both stood at my bedside. Stress was written all over their faces. They looked as if they hadn't slept in days. My always perfect mother wore a sweat suit with messy hair, and mascara-stained eyes. My father, who had always been the fortress of our family, looked broken and torn down.

"Oh, sweetheart, Tara's gone," my father stated as he rubbed the top of my head.

"Huh? What?" I said. That was when I realized that not even my parents could tell that I wasn't Mya, so my first instinct was to tell them the truth. "Daddy, I have to tell you something. I'm not—"

I was about to tell my father that there had been a mistake; that I was Tara and that Mya was the one who had been shot, but he interrupted me before I could finish.

"Shhh, don't talk right now, Mya. We are just glad that you're okay, honey," my father told me.

"Yes, dear. And as soon as you get out of here, we are going to go back to Detroit and forget about all of this sadness," my mother added.

Forget about all this? I thought as tears came to my eyes. How could they just forget about me and move on with their lives so quickly? Was I that forgettable?

My feelings were crushed and I cried uncontrollably. My parents thought that I was crying because of Mya's death, and a huge part of me was, but I was also crying because of their lack of sympathy. *They think I'm dead and they are already talking about moving on.* I decided that I would not ever tell my parents the truth. Why should I? The thought that the twin they hated had died and the one that they loved most had come out of this incident unscathed was the best news they could have received. For me to tell them that I was really alive, and that their pick was dead, would only add to my misery. So, on that day, I became Mya Evans. I decided to bury my secret when they buried my sister in the ground.

I boarded the plane back to Detroit with my parents by my side. They were so attentive and loving. I had never known them to be so caring, and I was already beginning to think that I had made the right decision. When we finally arrived back home, I felt a sense of relief wash over me. It was like a huge burden had been lifted off of my shoulders. The familiarity of everything around me was refreshing. Nobody knew how Mya's death affected me. There was a gap in my life that I would never ever be able to fill, although my parents tried to.

My mom and dad were with me night and day. I could tell that they were worried about what the death of my twin would do to me. I was keeping it together the best way that I could. I only showed my tears at night, and in the daytime I was silent. I withdrew into my thoughts, and the days right before the funeral were the worst.

Many people will never know the impression that they left on others, but I would get to see exactly what my friends thought of me now that they thought I was dead. I wondered who would show up at the funeral. I would get to see how they would react, hear the things that they said about me, and witness the tears they shed . . . if any at all.

The day finally came for me to say goodbye to Mya. I felt a little guilty for trying to take her place, and I wanted to tell my sister that I would do right by her name. I needed her to know that I loved her more than life itself, and I proved it by allowing everyone to bury 'Tara' instead of 'Mya.'

I stood between both of my parents as we entered the church. When the doors opened for us, I was surprised to see that each pew was filled with faces that I recognized. Some were family, others were friends, but there was absolutely no sitting room inside of the church. My parents had selected a beautiful white casket, and a collage full of my pictures was displayed next to all of the floral arrangements. I walked slowly toward the front and looked at Mya lying inside. She looked so pretty in her white Dolce dress. Her face was peaceful, and I silently thanked God that he had taken her instantly, because if she had suffered, it would have haunted me for the rest of my life.

I leaned over and kissed her cheek. "I love you, Mya," I said. "I love you so much and I will never forget you." It took me a while to walk away from her. It was the last time that I would ever see her again.

I sat down between my parents and my eyes roamed the room. I saw Summer and our eyes met. She was crying and she shook her head as she refocused on the front of the church. I smiled at the fact that she hurt over "my death" and I could not wait to talk to her. It had been so long since I had seen her. She was a true friend. Only now I would have to convince her to become Mya's true friend instead of Tara's.

Our community pastor delivered a beautiful sermon about a life that had ended too soon. My parents did not cry. They seemed to be so focused on keeping me sane that they were not even paying attention to the funeral. So I concluded that even at an event that was all about Tara, it was still all about Mya, their favorite daughter. Now that I had become Mya, everything would be okay and I could bury my neglected past.

We had a gathering at our house after the funeral and I was overwhelmed by all of the people that were there.

"Mya?" I wasn't used to responding to my sister's name yet, and I was so lost in my thoughts that I did not answer. "Mya?" Someone touched my shoulder and I jumped slightly.

"Oh!" I shouted. "You scared me!" I said as I turned around and stared at Maurice in the eyes. I smiled. It had been a few months since I had seen him, and just being in his presence seemed to wash all of my problems away.

"I'm sorry about Tara," he said. "She was a special girl. I cared about her, you know?" I could see him getting emotional, and I could not believe he was opening up to me about how he felt. Well, he wasn't actually telling me; he thought he was telling Mya.

"Thank you," I said shyly. I felt myself blush as I

thought of the kiss we had shared before I left. "You always know what to say."

He frowned at me and shook his head as if he was shaking sense into it. He wiped his growing facial hair with his hand and replied, "You sound just like her." He reached down and hugged me. I closed my eyes and enjoyed his embrace, until I heard someone clear their throat. I stepped back from him and saw Summer standing there with her arms crossed.

"Hi, Maurice," she said sadly. "I'm glad you decided to come. Tara would have wanted you here. She *really* liked you." Summer said her last line while staring at me, as if she felt she needed to remind me, the person she thought was Mya, that Maurice had been my sister's crush.

"I just wish I would have gotten a chance to know her a little bit better, Ma. She was supposed to be my girl," he said.

I blushed and changed the subject. "Hi, Summer," I said excitedly. I missed her so much and was glad to be around her again. She was my girl.

"Hey, Mya," she said. "I'm sorry about your sister. You know she was my girl, and no matter what you and I have been through, I want you to know that I loved Tara."

My eyes teared over and I replied, "I know you did, Summer. I hope we can be friends. It's very, very important for me to be cool with you. I want us to be friends."

Summer looked at me like I was crazy. "Mya, you know the deal. You might have all of these other girls intimidated by you, but you don't scare me. I could never be your friend again. I don't rock with chicks I don't trust. Your sister was like my sister. I'm only here for her and to pay my respect. You kept Tara down on purpose so that you could feel better than her. You never did like to share the spotlight; now she's gone and it is too late for you to make things right."

My chin hit the floor and I stormed off before I began to cry. I tried to mingle with some other people in the room, but Summer had dampened my spirits and I just wanted to be alone. Keeping my true identity a secret was going to be more difficult than I thought. It meant giving up my old life, my old friend—my only friend—and Maurice.

The days that followed were lonely. I was lonelier

than I had ever been before because I wasn't my-self. I couldn't be me, and the more I pretended to be Mya, the more I withdrew from my surround-ings. I was depressed all the time. With no Summer, no Maurice, and no real voice of my own, I felt trapped.

In school I learned that being Mya wasn't so easy after all. Yes, my sister was popular, but for the wrong reasons. People were used to being walked all over by Mya, and they seemed hesitant to interact with me when I treated them nicely. Mya had been cruel to a lot of people, and I found it exhausting having to fix the perceptions that Mya had built up for so long.

Still, no one at school was on to me. But my mother began to notice the difference.

"Mya, sweetheart, I think that you need to speak with someone about your sister's death," she said. "You're not taking it as well as we would like, and we just want you to be able to grieve in a healthy way."

"Do you miss her?" I asked. I had to know. It was eating me up inside that I could not tell my parents who I really was.

"Every day, Mya . . . every single day," my mother said.

If she was missing "Tara" so bad, then why wasn't she taking it just as hard as she felt I was? Why wasn't she grieving with me?

"If you need to talk about her, we can go to counseling as a family," my mother suggested. "I'm going to make some calls to see if we can meet with a family therapist tomorrow."

I didn't respond, but instead wondered how long I could keep up the façade. The last thing I needed was some shrink picking at my head, catching me off guard, catching me slipping. I knew I'd definitely have to be on my P's and Q's.

The next day in therapy, I sat across from my parents while our therapist sat behind his desk. Dr. Robert Nitz was one of Michigan's most renowned therapists, so I was afraid to talk to him. How could I hide the fact that I had taken my sister's identity from a man who was a professional at getting into people's heads? I fiddled with my fingers nervously, a habit that I always did when I was uncomfortable.

"So, tell me, what brings you all here?" Dr. Nitz

asked, looking back and forth from my mom and dad.

"We recently lost a member of our family," my father began. "Our daughters were twins, and one of them died a few weeks ago. We are worried that Mya here is not taking it too well." My father nodded toward me.

"What was your sister's name?" Dr. Nitz asked me.

"Tara," I whispered as I closed my eyes.

"And tell me about Tara," Dr. Nitz instructed as he wrote down notes on a pad.

I remained silent and my mother answered quickly. "Tara was beautiful. She was shy and delicate. We loved her—"

I smacked my lips and cut my mother off. "This is stupid. Can we go, please." I couldn't sit here and listen to my mother put on a front for this doctor.

"Why don't you like to talk about Tara?" Dr. Nitz asked me.

"I don't dislike talking about her. I just don't

think that I need help dealing with anything," I responded.

"Doctor, my wife and I are worried about Mya. Since her sister died, we have noticed a change, a drastic change in her." My father spoke timidly, as if he was afraid to insinuate anything about me. "I mean, I know twins have a special bond, and that dealing with death, period, is hard enough. But our Mya is like a whole other person."

"What types of changes have you noticed?" the doctor asked.

My father looked to my mother to answer.

"She has been taking on a lot of characteristics of Tara's," my mother said, putting her head down almost as if she were embarrassed.

I gasped, but remained silent as I listened to Dr. Nitz uncover our family issues.

"How so?" Doctor Nitz asked.

My mother sat up and responded, "Well, it's in her mannerisms and her personality. Tara used to be so happy, so carefree. Her pureness is what made her so special. Mya was always the attention seeker, but now that Tara is gone, I see Mya changing. I mean even the way she is playing with her fingers right now is something that her sister used to do."

As soon as my mother pointed it out, I forced myself to place my hands still in my lap. I could feel the pressure building behind my eyes.

"How do you feel, Mya?" the doctor asked. "Do you agree with your mother's observations? Do you feel you are trying to fill a void, the loss of your sister, by keeping certain parts of her here in your own special way?"

"It seems like they are noticing a lot now that Tara's gone," I said harshly. "Why did it take for her to die for them to notice things?"

The doctor looked a little puzzled at my response, then turned his attention to my mother and father for any clarity they could provide.

"Mya, we noticed everything about your sister," my father stated.

"No, you didn't. You didn't know her at all!" I protested. "You didn't even like her. You shipped her halfway around the world just to get rid of her. You split us up and now my sister is dead!"

My mother stood up and smacked me across the

cheek as her eyes burned with sadness. "How dare you, Mya. We have given you everything, sometimes at the expense of your sister. You will not talk to us like we are not good parents. You do not know the relationship that we had with Tara."

"Yeah, I do!" I hollered.

"You are her twin, but you don't know everything about her."

"I'm not her twin, Ma! The reason I know everything about Tara is because I am Tara! Don't you get it? I wasn't the one who died that night on the beach; Mya was. We switched necklaces. That's how everything got screwed up. I just let it stay that way because I wanted to know what it was like to be her. Everybody loved her. Even you and Daddy loved her more." I was breathing hard when I finished and my tears were endless. I was upset. This was my chance to get everything off of my chest.

"Oh, my God," my mother whispered. She looked at my father, who in turn stared intensely at me.

"Mya, this is not funny. This is cruel. How can you be so cruel?" he asked. "We will not accept this."

"Oh, my God," my mother said again. "I knew it. I knew it, Rich. I know my girls, and this is Tara."

Tears fell down her face as she stood and approached me. She reached her hand behind the back of my head and ran her fingers along my scalp. I knew what she was searching for. It was the only thing that I had that Mya did not. A scar. It was a scar that I had gotten when I was seven years old. I fell twenty feet out of my tree house and cracked my head wide open. I had to get several stitches, which had left a raised scar on my scalp. Eventually hair grew over it, but my mother never forgot about it. When she found what she was looking for, she withdrew her hand and gasped with her hand over her mouth.

"Tara?" she asked.

"Yes, Mommy, it's me," I cried. "I'm so sorry. I just wanted to come home. You and Daddy abandoned me. You sent me to California because you didn't want me. You always chose Mya over me. Everyone did. I just wanted you to love me."

Both of my parents surrounded me and hugged me tightly as I cried hysterically in their arms. My mother cried too, and my father consoled us both. We stayed that way for about ten minutes before Dr. Nitz interrupted us.

"Maybe the two of you need to explain to Tara why it is you sent her away," the doctor suggested.

"Tara, we are so sorry for making you feel like we didn't love you. We adore you, sweetheart. You are so beautiful on the inside and out. We never meant to choose favorites or make you feel like you had to compete with Mya. Your sister just needed a little more attention from us than you did," my father stated.

"But why? What made her so special?" I asked.

"Tara, Mya was sick. She had multiple personality disorder. We found out when you both were little girls. The reason we catered to her more is because we wanted to keep her healthy and try to help her get better. That is the reason why we would not tell her no for things that she asked for, or why we may have shown her more attention. It wasn't that we loved her more. She just needed us more.

"I know you noticed times when your sister could be cruel to you. There was a side of her that did not like you. She was envious of you, and one of her personalities threatened to harm you. She wrote it in her diary and we found it.

"We consulted with Dr. Nitz and he explained

that we should take her threat seriously. The real Mya loved you dearly, but when she wasn't herself, she could be very dangerous. We sent you to California to protect you, Tara. We only wanted the best for you. It was unfair to you and we are so sorry for making you feel like you didn't belong. We cherish you, Tara. You are our baby girl and we love you just as much as we loved Mya," my father explained.

I cried as I hugged them. How could I not have known this about my own sister? For so long I had been jealous of her, not knowing that she was really envious of me. This explained so much of Mya's behavior. I was so relieved that my parents had finally explained the reasons behind their actions. It made me feel like less of an outcast in my own family.

Slowly but surely, my parents and I worked through our pain. With the help of weekly visits to Dr. Nitz, we dealt with the death of my twin sister, the neglect I had felt growing up, and the reintroduction of me to our family and friends.

Summer cried a river when I told her the truth. I had missed her so much, and it was good to have my best friend back in my life. Maurice said that he always knew. He said that the way I acted gave me away. He told me that Mya had never been that nice before, and when I finally admitted my true identity to him, he immediately asked me to be his girl.

My life was finally what I had always wanted it to be. My parents and I could not have been closer. It seemed that everyone had noticed Mya's disposition except me. All of our friends told me that they were afraid to show me more attention than Mya out of fear that she may trip. Now I had friends and family who loved me. I just wished I could have had my sister in the picture to make it complete.

I regretted the fact that I had spent so much time being miserable and comparing myself to Mya. Once I got a chance to live her life, I learned that everything that glitters ain't always gold. The glitter of Mya's life had me blind to all of her flaws. The truth was, I wasn't Mya. I would never be Mya.

It took me some time to do, but I had finally found myself. I had learned to love me, and I was finally happy. I had accepted myself for who I was, and for the first time, I was proud of myself. I had developed my own self-esteem instead of living in my sister's shadow, and I had learned that it is always better to love yourself no matter what. I wouldn't let anyone else make me feel like I wasn't good enough. From this day forward, I'm just going to be me and do me. Forget all of the haters who try to stand in my way.

My name is Tara Evans, and if someone were to examine my life, they would think that I had it good—well, the truth is, they would be right.